# Bonnie Scotland

*Grace Greenwood*

# Contents

# BONNIE SCOTLAND

BY

Grace Greenwood

# ROBERT BURENS.

IT WAS on the evening of Sep-tember 23d, 1852, that I left dear old Ireland, with some kind Mends, for a short tour in " Bonnie Scotland." We took a steamer at Belfast for Ardrossan, where we landed early the next morning. Prom this port we went by railway to the town of Ayr, where we took a carriage and. drove over to the parish of Allo way, the birthplace of the poet Burns. Almost all travellers who visit Scotland come here,— some merely to have it to say that they have seen the place, with other sights, and some because of a real love for poets and poetry.

Robert Burns was a peasant, and the son of a peasant. His father's cottage, which we visited first, was in his time what is called in Scotland " a clay bigging," contain-ing only two apartments, a kitchen and a small sitting-room. We were sorry to find that an addition had been built on to it, and that it was occupied as an alehouse. There is a noble poem by Burns, entitled " The Cotter's Saturday Night," in which this cottage is described, as are also the pious father and mother of the poet.

Near by stands " old Alloway Kirk," a ruined stone church, also rendered fa-mous by a poem, though of a very different character, entitled " Tarn o' Shanter."

As this witty poem, like most of the writings of Robert Burns, is in the Scottish dialect, which my young readers would hardly understand, I will relate in plain prose the story, which made a great laugh through all the county of Ayrshire, some seventy-five years ago.

Tarn o' **Shanter,** which means Tom of Shan-ter, was a jolly peasant, who lived on a farm, in the poet's neighborhood. Tarn was unfortunately given to drinking too much, especially when he got away from home, among his cronies. His good wife, Kate, did her best to admonish and reprove him, and to warn him of the danger of such evil ways. She told him plainly that he was an idle, tippling, good-for-nothing fellow, who was bound to destruction as fast as he could post, in spite of the blessings of an industrious, affectionate wife, and a blooming family of little ones. She bade him mark her words, — that, sooner or later, he would be found drowned in the Doon; or that the witches and warlocks that haunted old Alloway Kirk would catch him and run off with him, body and soul, and she would be left a poor lone widow, and her sweet bairns be forever deprived of a father's care and example.

Well, One night, Tarn came home some time after twelve, with a fearful story of strange adventures, which for once stopped his Kate's scolding tongue with wonder and horror. It had been a market-day at Ayr, and Tarn was easily persuaded to stay late at the alehouse, by an old crony of his, one " Souter Johnny," or Shoemaker Johnny. The landlord and landlady sat down with them, and they drank the foaming ale, sung songs, and told stories, hour after hour, while the storm beat and the wind whistled without. At last, Tarn very reluctantly mounted his good gray mare, " Meg," and started for home ; — facing wind, rain, thunder, and lightning, but, as he afterwards declared, thinking them of small account, compared with the tempest which Kate would raise about his ears when he should reach his farm-house at Shanter.

As he drew near Kirk Alloway, which had long enjoyed the reputation of being haunted by very naughty spirits, what was his astonishment to see bright lights shining through its ruined windows, its cracks, and crannies, and to hear from it loud sounds of laughter, fiddling, and dancing!

Tam was no coward by nature, and the strong ale he had drunk made him wonderfully brave; so he did not hesitate to satisfy his curiosity by riding up to one of the windows, where he peeped in upon a startling scene. It was, he declared, a ball of lady and gentleman witches, with " Old Nick," in the shape of a horned beast, for fiddler!

The dancers were a wicked-looking set of creatures, — grim, ugly, and terrible, — who danced with wild leaps and furious yells, and made themselves as hideous and disgusting as possible. There was one exception, however; a young witch, called Nannie, tolerably good-looking, and who was so supple and frolicsome, bounded and whirled about so lightly, and took such prodigious jumps, that Tarn was delighted, and, forgetting where he was, and that he must not let that select company know that an uninvited guest was watching their unholy sport, he clapped his hands, and shouted, " Well done !"

As the poem says,—

"In an instant, all was dark!"

and out of the kirk poured the whole witch-company, shrieking and howling, and taking after Tarn, who spurred and whipped his faithful Meg to her utmost speed, in order to reach the bridge over the Doon; for those who believe in witches say that they have no power to cross running water. Thanks to Meg's fleet legs, he did escape from their clutches, but she, more Unlucky, came off second best, — for the spry witch Nannie caught her by the tail, and hung on till they reached the keystone of the bridge, when the tail gave way in her hands,

" And left poor Meggie scarce a stomp!"

When Tarn o' Shanter reached home, and related his fearful adventure to his wife Kate, she only said, " I told you so," and advised him to go to bed and sleep himself sober. I do not know that she doubted her husband's account of the awful sights he had seen and the peril he had been in; for she was an ignorant, superstitious woman, who believed in warlocks, witches, and all that sort of thing. Then, I think it likely he confirmed the strange tale he told, by pointing to the one, or rather the stump of the one poor Meg had lost; but some of his shrewd neighbors shook their heads and laughed, saying Tarn had had his mare docked in town, and had either imagined the witch-dance, from having drunk so much ale, or had invented the whole story to save himself from a sound rating, for staying so late, carousing with his roystering friends.

I cannot say which supposition is the true one, but I was told at Alloway that after Burns wrote *" Tarn o' Shanter, "* the hero of the ludicrous adventure never heard the last of it, and was laughed at to the day of his death, — as every idle, careless, beer-tippling story-teller deserves to be.

The old bridge over the Doon is still standing. We walked across it, and strolled up and down the green banks of the little river, repeating Burns's song,—

" Ye banks and braes o' bonnie Doon!"

A few rods away from tho bridge stands a noble monument, erected in honor of the poet. It overlooks nearly all the country which he loved and made famous, — which was called, by the right of his genius and fame, " the land of Burns," — though not a foot of it did he actually own while he lived.

The grounds about the monument are planted with beautiful trees, shrubs, and flowers, as though to keep green and sweet the memory of the departed poet.

We next visited a pretty cottage, all clambered over with roses, where we saw the Bister and two nieces of Robert Burns. Mrs. Begg was but a little girl when her brother died; but she remem-bered him perfectly well, and delighted to talk about him. She was a fine-looking, intelligent, agreeable old lady, and I was sorry to part with her and her interesting daughters.

We drove back to Ayr that afternoon, and took the evening train for Glasgow.

And now, that you may all more fully understand what renders Ayrshire, and especially Al-loway, so interesting to tourists, I will tell you something more of the poet-hero of that region, in a little sketch of

# THE LIFE OP ROBERT BURNS.

ROBERT BURNS was born on the 25th of January, 1759, in a little clay cottage, in the parish of Alloway, Ayrshire. His father, William Burns, was a farmer, — an honest, hard-working man, intelligent, and sincerely pious. His mother, Agnes Burns, was a gentle-hearted woman, rather more romantic and poetic in her tastes than her husband.

Very early in the life of her little Robert, Mrs. Burns perceived his genius, and reverenced it as a choice gift of God. Instead of trying to check his taste for poetry, lest it should be in the way of his getting on in the world as a peasant farmer, she kindly encouraged it, as something that might make the hard life of poverty beautiful and illustrious.

She had by heart a great many Scottish legends and poems, which she used to recite and sing to her noble boy. On many a stormy winter day, as she sat at her wheel, by the fireside, in their little cottage, she sung to him wild, sweet ballads, till his great, dark eyes would flash with fiery passion, or grow dim with tender tears.

Both father and mother labored diligently and constantly for the support and education of their children, whom they loved with the tenderest affection.

Robert and his brother Gilbert were early sent to school; and being boys of remarkable talent, and having an ardent desire to learn, they made rapid progress, and surpassed nearly all the other scholars.

Robert was a handsome boy, with a fine, sturdy frame; a well-formed head, proudly borne; a rich, glowing complexion; dark hair, large brown eyes, and a thoughtful, even serious expression of face; though, in his early manhood, he was renowned for wit and a reckless love of fun and frolic.

Poor Robert's schooling was soon over; and he was obliged, like his father, to labor incessantly at farming other people's land, — ploughing, planting, and harvesting, year after year, without a hope of earning more than a bare support. Mr. Burns continued very poor; his life was a constant struggle with want and care ; and it was the pleasure, as well as the duty of his sons, to give him all the aid in their power.

When Robert was about sixteen, he began to write poetry, — little, light, jingling songs at first, which did not cost him much effort, or take his thoughts long from his work, but which cheered and consoled him under his many toils and privations. Prom that time, he continued to write, more or less, and always better and better, till he died. For a long time, he had very little to encourage him, for he was nothing but an obscure ploughman; but he was conscious of noble feelings in his heart, and great thoughts in his brain, which the world needed to hear, and would listen to, and treasure up at last.

It would have been far better for himself and the world, if Robert Burns had never written anything but what his purest feelings prompted, and his conscience approved ; but I am sorry to have to tell you that, when he was about twenty-three, he fell in with some gay, unprincipled young men, who led him astray; and after that, he never was quite blameless in his life, and wrote some poems which do him no credit, and which he grieved to remember on his death-bed. When I think of his many good qualities,—his love and respect for his parents, his patient industry, his honesty and noble independence, — how I long to blot those miserable things out of the world, and out of everybody's memory forever!

At last the young poet published a volume of his writings, which made him so famous that he was invited up to Edinburgh, by some of the most celebrated people there. He spent a winter at the capital city, where he soon found himself a very great man indeed. Authors and scholars, lords and ladies, vied with each other as to who should honor and praise and feast him most. But through all this flattering attention from the rich and titled, he remained a plain, simple-hearted farmer, — true to his honest class, not striving to climb above it, or learning to despise it, — utterly without affectation and pretension. He was a little rustic in his manners, but never awkward, bashful, or cringing. He had learned from the mind and life of his good mother to respect and admire noble women, — so he knew how to address duchesses and countesses; he felt that he was a **man**, with a heart to love all high and beau-tiful things, an intellect to grasp and create grand thoughts, and a soul that must live on forever, with the life of God, — and he knew that the . proudest lord could be no more.

One day, when Robert Burns was dining with some literary people, he happened to be struck by some beautiful lines which were written underneath a picture, on the wall, and inquired who was the author of them. Nobody among the great folks present could answer the question; but finally, a quiet, fair-haired boy of fifteen, with a high, intellectual head, and thoughtful gray eyes, modestly gave the name of Langhorne as the writer. Burns turned and smiled upon the lad, with a look which he never forgot through all his own glorious life,—for that boy was Walter Scott.

It was supposed that some of the rich and powerful admirers of the " inspired Ayrshire ploughman," as they called Burns, would endeavor to place him in a comfortable and honorable situation, where he could devote the most of his time to literature. But no; he was only " the fashion " with them for a little while, and then they were after some other novelty. They gave him a few dinners, bought a few copies of his book, and then left him to struggle on for himself, in the old way. The next year he solicited the influence of his best friend among the nobility, Lord Glencairn, to obtain a situation in the Excise ; yet, for some reason or other, his request was not granted. But another friend, Mr. Alexander Wood, a surgeon, still affectionately spoken of in Edinburgh as " Kind Old Sandy Wood," a far better title than " Earl" or " Duke," hearing of the poet's wish, quietly went and procured him the appointment. The duty of an Exciseman is to arrest smugglers and. the unlicensed manufacturers and sellers of liquor, — not a very pleasant, proper, or profitable business for the poet, but it was the best that offered then: he accepted it gratefully, and always faithfully discharged the duties of his office.

He returned to the country, married a young woman whom he had long loved, named Jean Armour, and settled down upon a farm, at Ellies-land, near Dumfries. Here he was very happy for several years with his dear wife and children, and here he wrote some of his noblest poems. But his farm proved unproductive, his writings brought him but little money, and he was finally obliged to sell out, remove to Dumfries, and depend entirely on his office as Exciseman.

In December, 1795, he lost his only daughter, a little girl of whom he was very fond, and about that time his own health began to fail alarmingly. Riding over the country in all seasons and weather gave him rheumatic fever, from which he never wholly recovered. During the spring and early summer of 1796 he was obliged to resign his business, which was a great sorrow to him, as he thus lost the larger part of his salary, and he feared that his family must suffer without it. On the 5th of July he went to the sea-side, hoping to get better there,—but it did him no good. On the 7th he wrote to his dear brother, Gilbert: " I am dangerously ill, and not likely to get better. God keep my wife and children!" On the 18th he came home to die, and on the 21st he died.

Mrs. Burns was left with four little sons; but the last práyer of the husband and father for his dear ones was heard, and God *did* " keep " them. He raised up friends to care for them, so that they never came to want. Mrs. Burns lived to a good old age, and found herself honored more and more, every year, as the widow of a great poet. Two of her sons are yet living, and are very much beloved and respected.

It is about sixty-four years since Robert Burns died, and now his name is known and his songs are sung the wide earth over,—which proves that when God gives a man true genius, all the neglect, poverty, and trouble in the world cannot keep it down. Yet there were many who would have lived and died happier, if, when they had the opportunity, they had given good counsel and brotherly aid to poor Burns, and, above all, comforted him on his death-bed, with the promise that his family should not be friendless when he was gone.

Dear children, when you read or hear sung " Auld lang Syne," " Bonnie Doon," " Highland Mary," " John Anderson," and other of the sweet songs of Robert Burns,

I am sure you will think gently of the poet, —will pity him for his errors, as well as for his misfortunes, and feel admiration and gratitude for one who, out of a troubled life and a sorrowful heart, made so much music for the world.

# SIR WILLIAM WALLACE.

LASGOW is considered the third city of Great Britain in wealth, population, commerce, and manufactures. It is situated in Lanarkshire, on the river Clyde, at the point where it becomes navigable to the Atlantic Ocean.

This city is said to have been founded as early as 560, by St. Kentegern, who appears to have been remarkably active and enterprising for a Churchman. Very little is known of the early history of Glasgow, except as connected with its famous minster, founded in the reign of King David the First, in 1136, and standing yet. It is a dark, imposing edifice, more stupendous than beautiful, and chiefly remarkable as being the only cathedral in the realm which escaped destruction in the Reformation. The Protestants of Glasgow, very much to their credit, unceremoniously declared against the demolition of the . building; but they made a sort of burnt-oflering to the spirit of the Reformation, of the pictures and- images of the saints, of altars and confes-sionals.

After it passed into the hands of the Reformers, it was called the " High Kirk," or church; and, once upon a time, it occurred to the session, or leading men, that it would be convenient and comfortable to have seats, to sit upon during the long sermons of their divines. So they had made what are called "forms," for the male part of the congregation; surlily forbidding the women to make use of them ; saying, that if they wished to sit down during service they might bring stools from home, — good enough seats for them. I should like to see " the brethren " of any church, in our age, and especially in our country, attempt to carry matters over "the sisters" with such a high hand!

But these were disagreeable, troublesome times to live in, when the men were not only ungallant toward the women, but quarrelsome among themselves. They all went armed everywhere,—even clergymen wore daggers and small-swords into the pulpit, where they professed to teach the mild and merciful religion of Christ.

Glasgow is now a handsomely built city, with many fine public edifices, and pleasant, open squares, and several noble monuments. But it is a place of little historical or romantic interest, and tourists do not often linger in it long. We left the day after our arrival, without the unpleasant feeling which we often experienced in going from other places, that we left many things unseen which could not be seen elsewhere.

The first object of interest on our route was Dumbarton Rock, grandly towering up at the point of junction of the Clyde and the Severn,— crowned by its imposing stronghold, so often mentioned in history, and most sadly memorable as having once been the prison of Sir William Wallace, about whom I shall say more by and by.

Dumbarton Rock is one of those places which seem to have been formed by nature for the sites of castles and fortresses. It rises five hundred and sixty feet above the sea, in several bare, jagged, defiant points, apparently utterly impregnable, and yet its very supposed security was once the cause of the castle being surprised and taken, in a very singular and daring way, which I would like to describe to you, if I had the space; but I have not.

We took a steamer up Loch Long, an arm of the sea. The scenery along this loch, or lake, is very striking and picturesque, though less so than that of Loch Goil, which branches off from it. I never shall forget my delight in sailing up this beautiful sheet of water. The shores on either side are now bold, precipitous, and rocky, now clothed with luxuriant foliage, dense, dark woodlands, or lovely green lawns, sloping down to the water.

Loch Goil is the scene of Campbell's pathetic ballad of " ***Lord Ullin's Daughter***

At the head of Loch Goil we took a coach, and drove several miles through a wild, romantic glen, to a place, called St. Catherine's, where we crossed another lovely lake, Loch Fyne, to the town of Inverary.

The most interesting sight at Inverary is the Castle of the Duke of Argyle. This is a very handsome and stately building, but rather modern in its style. After all the palaces and castles we had seen, this did not strike us as being outwardly or inwardly very grand or wonderful. But, according to the old Scotch housekeeper, who shows visitors through the rooms, there is nothing in all the world to be compared to " the *Dook's* braw castle." I have my doubts whether she would admit that Solomon's famous temple approached it, in magnificence. In one of the state apartments there is some very beautiful tapestry, which the old lady solemnly affirms was woven by no human hands, but by " goblins, wha are a' deid noo," — (who are all dead now). It was only a fine specimen of the celebrated Gobelin tapestry, made in France.

We enjoyed highly our strolls through the noble park and gardens of the castle, and a charming view from *Duniquoich*, a lofty hill, or, as 1 heard it called, " a young mountain," on the Duke's estate.

The following morning we took a carriage, and posted through Glencoe, a grand, dark mountain pass, to Tarbet, on Loch Lomond. After strolling about the romantic shores, seeing some new beauty at almost every step, we crossed the lake in a row-boat, to Rowardennan Inn, where we took ponies to ascend Ben-Lomond. This is a very respectable mountain, rising three thousand two hundred and ten feet above the lake. The distance from the Inn to the summit is full six miles, and we found the way either boggy and slippery, or steep and rocky; — yet our brave little ponies were fully equal to it, and seemed to enjoy the climb almost as much as we.

O, the vast and wonderful prospect which we looked down upon at last! Lakes, rivers, valleys, glens, castles, parks, cities, and a countless host of mountains, stretching away to the north, like the dark, mighty waves of a great sea heaved up in a midnight storm.

But the sublime emotions which these grand views excited in our minds, did not prevent us from keenly enjoying the fan of our descent from this lofty height. Our ponies, refreshed by a long rest, and by browsing upon the summit, went galloping, leaping, and plunging down at a right jolly rate, and dashed into the yard of the little inn in fine style.

The story which I shall tell you in this number is sad and tragical, but I hope it will interest you as the life of an illustrious patriot and a brave man.

# THE STORY OF SIR WILLIAM WALLACE.

Edward the First of England, a powerful and warlike monarch, as you may remember, after the death of King Alexander the Third, boldly usurped the government and conquered the kingdom of Scotland. He was in fact the sovereign, though he declared the weak John Baliol his " vassal-king," and had him crowned at Scone, under that inglorious title. He placed English garrisons in all the Scottish castles, and left the entire management of the country in the hands of Englishmen, who proved themselves hard and insolent rulers,—burdening with taxes, insulting and tyrannizing over the Scots, till that proud and stern people became thoroughly enraged against them. Yet for a long time they brooded over their wrongs in silence and inactivity, hav-ing no one popular leader under whose command they could hope to avenge them, and recover the lost liberties of their country.

At last the man for the times came forth,— not from the old Scottish nobility, but from the middle classes. William Wallace was the son of Sir Malcolm Wallace, of Ellerslie, Renfrewshire. While yet a boy, his father and elder brother were killed, in fighting against the English; and thus his heart was early embittered toward the usurpers and invaders.

At that time the Scots were a very rude people, — in many respects scarcely more than half civilized ; but they were brave, resolute, and hardy, and had been gifted by nature with a peculiar, passionate love of freedom. The men of mountainous countries are not the stuff that slaves are made of, — being generally fierce,

determined, and indomitable, and seeming to possess something of the fixedness of
" the everlasting hills," and the spirit of the wild winds and the eagles that sweep
about their summits. It had cost King Edward an immense amount of trouble, blood,
and money to conquer Wales and Scotland; and, after all, he never could feel secure
for a day that they would have the decency to stay conquered.

When matters in Scotland appeared to promise most favorably for the new
English government, as the nation seemed finally crushed into submission, there
was a certain young lad quietly pursuing his education in Stirlingshire, who was
destined to give his Majesty no little annoyance. This was William Wallace.

As Wallace grew into manhood, he became remarkable for his personal strength
and beauty. He was fair-haired, blue-eyed, tall, straight, and athletic. His disposi-
tion was mild, generous, and amiable ; and it is probable that, had it not been for
his peculiar wrongs, and the wrongs and sufferings of the common people, — with
whom he had deep sympathy, — he might have led always a quiet and peaceable
life.

While he was yet very young, he was insulted and attacked by an English officer in Dundee, and, in self-defence, killed his antagonist. He was then proscribed,
and took refuge in Ayrshire; where, collecting a force of brave countrymen about
him, he waged an irregular warfare against all the English who came in his way,
punishing them summarily for every act of rapine and cruelty toward the poor and
defenceless. He soon rendered himself notorious by his bold exploits, not only in
Ayr, but throughout the neighboring shires; and many high-spirited men joined
him, thinking it better to live the perilous life of an outlaw than the shameful life
of a slave.

He afterwards retired to the forest recesses of Clydesdale, where he made himself more and more formidable to the English,—more and more beloved by the
poor Scots. At any time, the sound of his bugle could summon recruits from the
hamlets around him, and his band of regular followers daily increased. These were
all called " Robbers" by their enemies ; but, instead of being so, they were mostly

gentlemen of respectable old Scottish families, who had been robbed and outraged by the shameless invaders,

At length William Wallace became so powerful and renowned that the English tried in many ways to buy him over to their interest. They offered him wealth, high position, and titles, if he would follow the example of most of the nobles and gentry of Scotland, and swear allegiance to Edward. But he proudly answered, that no money could buy his honor; that for no position at the court of a tyrant would he exchange his life of hardship and peril in the free forest-land; that no title was so noble as that of an honest man.

A cruel sorrow and wrong finally determined Wallace to take a yet more decided and prominent part against the merciless enemies of his country. On one of his venturous visits to Lanark he met a beautiful young orphan girl, by the name of Marion Bradfute. When he went home he found he could not forget her,—that her sweet face was always before him, and that he was no longer happy in his wild, lonely life. After a good deal of doubt and hesitation,—for the generous hero felt that he ought to devote himself entirely to his country, and not think of the peaceful joys of love and home, —he sought the lovely orphan, and left the matter with her to decide. She thought that he might be soldier, patriot, and husband at the same time, and, being a brave girl, she loved him for his heroic resistance to oppression, and, though he was proscribed as an outlaw, was not afraid to become his wife. They were married, but privately, and Wallace was obliged to use great caution in visiting his bride, as it would endanger his life to be recognized at Lanark. Another reason for secrecy lay in the fact that the English governor, a hard, brutal man, by the name of Hazlerigg, had fixed upon Marion as a wife for his son,—because of her wealth, she being an heiress to considerable property, — thus the knowledge of her marriage with Wallace would doubly enrage him.

One fatal day Wallace was recognized and attacked by some English soldiers, in the street near his own house. He fought bravely, but was about to be overpowered by numbers, when . his door opened and a fair hand beckoned him to a temporary shelter. He dashed into his house, and escaped through a back door into the woods behind. It did not occur to his own tender, manly heart, that his devoted wife would be called to pay for his life with her own ; yet so it was. Hazlerigg arrested Marion, and, having ascertained that she was the wife of Wallace, put her to death.

This savage deed filled all hearts with indignation and horror. The fearful tidings were carried to poor Wallace, who, half distracted by grief and anger, collected his band, marched to Lanark, killed the monster Hazlerigg, and drove the English from the town.

From this time Wallace devoted himself yet more entirely and solemnly to the great work of redeeming his oppressed country, and I fear— for Wallace, with all his pure and lofty spirit, was but human, and lived in bloody times — swore a fearful oath to avenge, to the utmost, his own terrible wrongs.

At length the whole country became thoroughly aroused,—there were revolts occurring in all directions, and so many nobles and other men of note flocked to the standard of Wallace, that King Edward sent a large army to put the rebels down again. The first great battle of Wallace was fought at Cambuskenneth, near the bridge of Stirling, where the English were completely defeated and routed.

Soon after this, the Scots conferred upon Wallace the title of " Guardian of Scotland, in the name of King John Baliol." This was a sort of regency, and excited some enmity among the Scottish nobility; but Wallace bore himself with much prudence and modesty, and never sought to be anything more than the servant of the people he so much loved. But he remained in prosperity and power, and the nation in peace, but about a year. It seemed that the Scots were not yet worthy of freedom, at least the nobles were not. They felt, or affected to feel, a mean contempt for Sir William Wallace, because he was not a man of high rank, and insolently rebelled against his authority. At the battle of Falkirk, they who formed the cavalry fled at the first onset of the English, and, through their cowardly defection and the great superiority of the enemy, Wallace and his gallant infantry were defeated.

This was a terrible reverse of fortune; but the Scots did not give up the struggle for several years, gaining some advantages against tremendous odds, but not succeeding as they would have done had they unanimously placed Wallace at the head of affairs, reposing perfect confidence in his judgment and patriotism.

At length King Edward, by force or bribery, reconquered one after another of the leaders, and band after band of the dispirited army, till Sir William Wallace and his followers were the only true freemen in Scotland, — they alone having refused to take the oath of allegiance, and servilely submit themselves to the hated usurper. The hero, saddened and disappointed, but not broken in spirit, or quite despairing, retired to his old haunts among the forests and mountains, and his old outlaw life, — again summoning his faithful adherents, again alarming his enemies with his bold bugle-blast. Thus he lived for more than seven years, laying plans for his country's deliverance, and patiently waiting for an opportunity to carry them out.

But the same God who inspires patriots and martyrs, in his mysterious providence permits the existence of traitors and betrayers. A soldier and a Scotchman was at last found mean and miserable enough to betray Sir William Wal-lace, and sell himself to eternal infamy, for the reward offered by the English. This was one Sir John Monteith, who treacherously got possession of him and delivered him up to his en emies, on the 5th of August, 1305.

After a short imprisonment in Dumbarton Castle, Wallace was conveyed to London, and was tried in Westminster Hall, charged with high treason. To this charge he simply replied, "I could not be a traitor to Edward, for I never was his subject."

During this trial the noble prisoner was, like his Divine Master, crowned in mockery,—being compelled to wear a garland of green leaves, as the king of robbers and outlaws.

He was condemned to death,-—drawn in a sledge to the scaffold, and beheaded. His body was then divided into four quarters, and stuck upon pikes on London bridge.

Little is known of the last hours of Wallace, except that he died bravely, yet meekly,—protesting that he had done nothing for his country of which he repented, and that he only regretted not having accomplished more.

Edward the First doubtless thought that he had struck down the spirit of Scottish freedom, with the life of its noblest champion. But freedom is an immortal principle, planted by God in the heart of man, and nothing can utterly uproot and destroy it. The rich blood of Wallace seemed to water and nourish it into a new growth,—his name became doubly dear, as that of a martyr to liberty, and grew to be the sacred watchword of his struggling countrymen. To this day it is more honored and beloved than that of any monarch — with the exception, perhaps, of Robert Bruce—that ever sat on the throne of Scotland.

I have not, like the historians, given you the details of the fierce skirmishes and bloody battles in which Wallace was engaged,—for my heart is not in such things. It seems to long more and more, day by day, for that blessed time of " peace and good-will" promised to us, when "the nations shall learn war no more," but dwell on the quiet, happy earth like one great family, — like the children of God, as they are. But because Sir William Wallace did the best and noblest he knew how, in the dark and troublous times in which he lived,—because he was generous, brave, true, and self-sacrificing., even to death, — I deeply reverence his memory, and have had a heart-felt pleasure in writing out his story.

Lochs Lomond and Katrine.

# ROB ROY.

OCH LOMOND is considered the finest of all the Scottish lakes. It is twenty-three miles in length, and five in breadth at the widest, and contains a multitude of the most lovely and fairy-like islands you can imagine. The scenery of its shores is wonderfully beautiful and grand, — now filling the heart with delight, now thrilling it with awe, or lifting it in loving gratitude to God, who has placed us in a world of so much beauty and sublimity, and gifted us with souls to enjoy and reverence the works of his hands.

The day of our trip up this lake was delightful. A soft autumnal sun goldened all the landscape, and the blue waves danced in a light, pleasant wind, while the atmosphere was so clear that we could see to a great distance. To the northward, the dark, lofty mountains; to the southward, a fair, fertile country; on either side, shady and flowery islands, or noble shores, with rocks, crags, and caves; smooth, grassy slopes, or abrupt, heathery heights.

I remember a little incident of this trip, trifling enough, but which struck me at the time. I observed a large hawk hovering in the air, near our boat, and circling lower and lower. Suddenly he darted downward, and caught a fish from the water. He then began to ascend rather slowly, impeded by the weight of his prey. It happened that there was on board a Scotch duke, who had been sporting in the Highlands, and who now, having his fowling-piece loaded, took a shot at the bold marauder, and, it seemed, slightly wounded him, for a few feathers floated lightly down the air; he gave a hoarse scream, and, in his pain or fright, dropped the fish, which fell, apparently lifeless, into the lake. Scarcely, however, had it touched the water, when the indomitable hawk was after it again! He caught it in his talons, and bore it off in triumph, screaming down a democratic defiance to the duke. I remember saying, that none but a Highland hawk would be so courageous and persevering.

We landed at Inversnaid, on the east shore of the lake, and drove through a rough, narrow glen, about five miles long, to Loch Katrine. On our way we passed the ruins of Inversnaid fort, erected to check the famous outlaw-chief Bob Boy Macgregor, and a forlorn Highland cabin, in which his wife, Helen Macgregor, was born.

Loch Katrine is most famous as the principal scene of Scott's charming poem, " The Lady of the Lake;" but its beauty would alone distinguish it above nearly all other lakes. It is only about ten miles long, and at no place more than two broad.

A mere pond, compared with our great inland seas, it is surely not grand, yet the scenery which surrounds it is some of the grand-est, as well as the most enchanting, in the world.

We descended Loch Katrine by the tiniest steamer I ever voyaged upon; whose speed was proportional to her size. She passed over the little waves with little nervous jumps, puffed out a little column of smoke, and left an exceedingly little wake behind her. Yet we reached the most beautiful and romantic part of the lake at a very favorable time,—just at sunset, when mountain, stream, island, rock, and green winding shore were bathed and glorified in gorgeous lights of purple and gold.

Near the eastern shore is " Ellen's Isle," a charming spot, particularly interesting to the admirers of " The Lady of the Lake." A little way beyond Loch Katrine lie " The Trosachs," or "bristled territory," a wild, mountainous country, through which winds the dark defile of " Beal-an-Duine," the place where, according to the poem, the " gallant gray " of Fitz-James sunk down and died.

Loch Lomond, Loch Katrine, and the country around, are closely associated with the melancholy and romantic history of the Macgregors, of whom I will try to give you a clear though brief account.

# THE CLAN MACGREGOR, AND THE STORY OF ROB ROT.

The Highlands of Scotland have been, for many centuries, inhabited by a remarkable race of people, called Celts; naturally hardy, proud, and warlike, and descended from the ancient Britons, who took refuge in that almost unknown country at the time when the Romans invaded and conquered Great Britain. To this day they have a distinct language, the Gaelic, utterly unlike the English or the Scotch dialect of the Lowlands. Their dress is very peculiar and picturesque; but, as you have all doubtless some idea of this from pictures, I will not stop to describe it.

The Highlanders, in old times, were divided into distinct tribes, or " clans." Now-a-days they keep up the names of these, but the old system of clanship, with its distinguishing customs and prejudices, has almost utterly passed away.

All the members of each of these clans believe themselves descended from one great ancestor, and were generally called by his name, with the addition of *Mac*, which signifies sons. Each clan had its chief, supposed to be a descendant, in the most direct line, of the founder of the family. This chief they all implicitly obeyed, even when to do so was to go against their own wishes and rebel against the king.

These different clans occupied distinct mountain districts, and were far enough, I am sorry to say, from dwelling in peace with each other or their common enemy, the Lowlanders. Indeed, they were such a bold, belligerent people, that it might be said of them, that they were never happy, except when in trouble and tumult, — never content, except when fighting and marauding. Yet they had their own good qualities. They were brave, enduring, liberty-loving, trustworthy, hospitable, and unrivalled in their loyal devotion to their hereditary chiefs, and those they recognized as their rightful sovereigns, especially (which was noblest of all) when those sovereigns were in difficulty. The most remarkable of the Highland clans, in character and history, were the Macgregors, descendants of Gregor, son of Kenneth Mao-Alpine, King of the Scots and Picts. This takes them back a long way; and, indeed, the Mac-gregors made a great boast of their antiquity, saying, that " Hills, waters, and MacAlpines were the oldest things in Albion."

They were a proud, powerful, and wealthy clan down to the time of King Robert Brace, when their reverses and persecutions began. That monarch, whom they had not favored, undertook, in the height of his power, to check and humble them, by depriving them of a large portion of their possessions. Prom that time, misfortunes and wrongs thickened upon their heads, but without dismaying or subduing them. All the other clans submitted to the king, and received from him charters for their lands, but the Macgregors scorned to secure themselves by such concessions.

In the fifteenth century it was proclaimed that their territory had all been bestowed upon their enemies, the Campbells. But they stood sturdily upon their lands, and bade the new owners come and take possession if they dared! They were too powerful to be driven off; yet, having lost their legal rights, they were regarded as aliens and outlaws, and persecuted by all their neighbors. They obstinately refused to recognize their new landlords, desperately opposed all the forces sent against them, and made frequent and destructive incursions into the territory of their foes. They divided into two separate bands, one on the banks of Loch Rannoch, the other living in the neighborhood of Loch Lomond; there firmly planting themselves, and standing, like hunted wild animals, at bay.

Through reign after reign, and century after century, they continued to be a doomed, persecuted, and suffering, but unconquerable people, — clinging to their old homes, fighting and harassing their old enemies, the Campbells and Men-zies, till the chiefs of those clans began to think that, but for the name of the thing, they might as well not have such an unruly and profitless set of tenants.

The reign of James the Sixth was perhaps their darkest time. Then, for the slaughter of the Colquhouns and Buchanans at Glenfruin, or the Glen of Sorrow, a royal decree was passed abolishing forever the name and clan of Mac-gregor.

All that bore that surname were commanded to exchange it for some other, or suffer death, and every man was forbidden to wear arms. Those who rebelled against these severe laws were hunted down like beasts, by their old enemies, now in the employ of the king, and assisted by the royal troops. Through a long series of years, law after law was passed, bearing harder and harder upon them, till it was a wonder their very souls were not crushed out of them by oppression, The most brutal of all, was one com-manding their women to be branded with the mark of a key in the face; but I believe that no one was ever found bold or cruel enough to execute this law.

During the civil wars of Cromwell, the Mac-gregors rallied and fought bravely for King Charles, notwithstanding all the wrongs inflicted on them by his father, James the Sixth. On the restoration of Charles the Second, they were allowed to reassume their ancient name, and were again recognized as an independent clan. After the English Revolution, the hard laws against them were revived, but never very strictly carried out, — and as the civil wars of the two countries came to an end, the persecutions of this unfortunate clan gradually ceased.

The story of Rob Roy is told in full, in Scott's Novel by that name, and in the introduction to that work. I can only give you a slight sketch of the character and life of this last hero of the Macgregors.

Rob Roy Macgregor CAMPBELL, as he was obliged to call himself, was descended from one of the ancient chiefs of the proscribed clan, who lived at Glengyle, on Loch Lomond. He was born in comparatively peaceful times, received a good education, and was bred to a respectable calling. He married Helen Macgregor, of Inver-snaid, and for several years led an industrious and blameless life, never dreaming of being anything but an honest and peaceable man. His occupation was that of cattle-dealer, — collecting cattle in the Highlands and driving them to markets in the Lowlands, or to England.

It happened, unluckily, that Rob once entered into a partnership with the Duke of Montrose, in a great cattle speculation, which turned out very badly. Rob came home from England almost ruined, as he had invested his all; and when he went to settle with the Duke, that ignoble nobleman insisted on having back every penny of the money he had risked, with the interest! This, of course, could not be; Rob offered him his share of the little that was left, which he would not accept, but advertised the unfortunate drover as a swindler and a thief, and offered a reward for his apprehension as a culprit.

This finished the ruin of the Macgregor; he fled to his native hills and glens, and took up the life of an outlaw and freebooter.

The Duke of Montrose seized upon Rob's property of Craigroyston; his men sold all the stock and furniture, and even insulted and abused Helen Macgregor, — a proud and passionate woman, who, with her husband, from that day swore vengeance against Montrose and his party.

Rob Roy soon found himself at the head of a formidable band of Macgregors, who had their own wrongs to avenge, and their own living to get, by desperate means. Their robberies were principally of cattle, and they were called ***cear-nochs,*** or " cattle-lifters." Rob said that he was only carrying on his old business in a new way.

Rob himself was a generous and benevolent freebooter, — if such a thing can be, — and very like the English Robin Hood, — often taking from the abundance of the rich to supply the needs of the poor. He believed that he had been cruelly driven into his lawless life, and often declared that he would much prefer a more honorable and peaceable career. In the Rebellion of 1715 he took the side of the Stuarts, and had a commission in the rebel army. But when that rash enterprise failed, he was obliged to return to his old haunts, when he again devoted himself to the great business of his life, — tormenting the Duke of Montrose. Two or three times the Duke made out to capture the outlaw; but just as he was rejoicing over his good luck, Rob slipped, eel-like, out of his hands. Once he built a fort at Inversnaid, to protect the country against the bold robber, and distributed arms among his tenants ; but Rob very soon routed the garrison, and got possession of every one of the Duke's muskets.

As Rob Roy grew to be an old man, he felt a stronger desire to return to an honest way of living. He had an idea of resuming cattle-dealing, and redeeming his reputation! He even addressed a petition to one of King George's officers for pardon and permission to take his forfeited place in society, without danger of arrest and death. This touching request was taken no notice of, and poor Rob was obliged to die an outlaw. He died in the year 1738, a very old man, professing the Christian's hope. Just before he breathed his last, he requested his piper to play the mournful Gaelic dirge, — ***Ha til mi tulidh***, — "We return no more."

He was buried in the old churchyard of Bal-quidder. No name is on the tombstone, but a broadsword is carved upon it, as a sign of his fierce spirit and lawless life. Yet he seems to rest as tranquilly as any innocent babe in all the churchyard ; the birds are not afraid to sing above his grave, nor the grass and flowers to creep over it; neither do dews and sunbeams refuse to descend upon it.

So, as the bold robber-chief seemed subdued and humble at the last, may we not hope that he yielded himself, like an erring but repentant child, to his God, and that Divine peace and forgiveness rested on his soul.

The lesson, dear children, which I would draw from these old stories of wars, tumults, wrongs, and oppressions, is a grateful trust in the steady advance of the world toward a time of peace, justice, and brotherhood. True, there are wars now,— sad, terrible wars,—but they are between rival nations, not bitter, bloody strifes between clan and clan, family and family. The clans of Scotland now dwell in perfect peace, indeed are almost merged together, and it would now be as impossible for any one of them to be unjustly persecuted, as that any man should be driven to the life of an outlaw because of a failure in a business undertaking. When you hear unhappy, croaking people say, " Ah me! the world is getting worse and worse! "don't believe them. It is constantly growing better, and the nations are slowly drawing nearer to each other, and so, to God. Yet, there is room enough for improvement, and it is not for us to be puffed up with our civilization and righteousness.

We look back with pity and horror to the hunted and half-barbarous Macgregors of two or three hundred years ago; but they had some noble qualities, which would put to the blush too many in our enlightened times. In proof of this, I will relate

# A LITTLE STORY.

One morning a young Macgregor, the son of an old chieftain residing at Clenurchy, went out, with a party of his clansmen, to shoot on the moors. During the day they fell in with a young gentleman by the name of Lamont, and toward night invited him to go with them to an inn, for some refreshment. All went very pleasantly and merrily for some time, and then a quarrel arose, about some trifle, between young Macgregor and the stranger, over their wine. In a moment, swords were drawn, and at the first pass Macgregor fell dead! Lamont made his escape and fled, but was fiercely pursued by the friends of the man he had slain. All night long he ran through the wild Highland country, and in the morning sought refuge at the first house he saw. An old man was standing at the door. " Save my life ! " panted out Lamont;. " I am pursued by enemies."

" Whoever you are, you are safe here," replied the old man, taking him in, and commending him to his wife and daughters. But presently the Macgregors came up, and told the generous host that his only son had fallen in a quarrel, and that he was harboring the murderer! For a moment, the poor old father bowed his face in his hands, crying out bitterly, " O my son! my son!" His wife and daughters burst into sobs and shrieks ; the clansmen pressed forward, with curses and threats, toward Lamont, who gave himself up for lost, when the chieftain sternly waved them back, saying: " Be quiet; let no man touch the youth ! He has the Macgregor's word for his safety, and, as God lives, he *shall* be safe while he is in my house."

He faithfully kept his word; and even accompanied Lamont to Inverary, with a guard, and having landed him on the other side of Loch Fyne, said: " Lamont, you are now safe, if you keep out of the way of my clan. I can no longer protect you. Farewell, and may God forgive you."

The happiest part of this story is, that when a new persecution of tho Macgregors broke out, and the old chief of Clenurchy was driven from his property, he and his family wore offered a home in the house of Lamont, who ever after devoted himself to the work of atoning to the poor exiles for the wrong he had done them.

Dear children, let us bless the good God who, in all ages and in all countries, has implanted such generous and beautiful sentiments in the human heart.

Stirling Castle.

# THE LITTLE DOUGLAS.

E TRAVELLED from the Tro-sachs to Stirling by the stage-coach, taking out-side seats, so as to have better views of the lovely and noble country through which we passed.

The most interesting object on our way was the ruined castle of Doune, on the banks of the Teith, once one of the proudest strongholds in all Scotland. It was built by Murdock, Duke of Albany, who was afterwards, with his two sons, beheaded upon Stirling Castle-hill, from which he could see " the bannered towers " of his princely residence.

The old town of Stirling is grandly situated on an eminence, near the river Forth, — but contains nothing of remarkable interest, except the castle, which stands on the highest point, overlooking the country for a great distance, in every direction. Within sight from its walls are no less than three of the most celebrated of Scotland's battle-fields, — Cambuskenneth, Falkirk, and Bannockburn.

Stirling Castle is now only kept up as a fortress, but throughout the reigns of the Stuarts it was a favorite and important royal residence. Among the interesting objects and places which were pointed out to us by the soldier who conducted us through the old palace and castle, was the room in which King James the Second killed, with his own hand, the Earl of Douglas, — an unprincely and most inhos-pitable act; though this Earl, like the greater portion of his family, was ambitious, unscrupulous, cruel, and rebellious.

We were also shown a narrow road, descending the precipice behind the castle, and called **Bal-langeich**, which signifies in Gaelic," windy pass."

James the Fifth used to pass out of the Castle by this way, when he went on secret expeditions, in disguise, as he was very fond of doing, — and he took a name from it, calling himself, ***"the Guidman, of Ballangeich"*** [1] He was a merry, daring prince, a sort of Scotch Haroun Alraschid, and had many amusing adventures under his assumed character, — one or two of which I will relate

One time, when the king had distinguished foreign guests, and was feasting them with great state and jollity at Stirling, he was informed by his steward that provisions were running rather low, and sent off in haste to the hills for venison. The hunters were successful in killing a fine lot of fat deer, which they slung upon the backs of horses, and set out for Stirling.

It happened, unluckily for them, that they were obliged to pass the Castle of Arnpryor, in the district of Kippen, the seat of one of the Buchanans,— a rude, in-dependent, and care-for-naught

[1] "Goidman" signifies farmer.

Highland chief. It happened, also, that this laird was entertaining a large com-pany, and, like the king, had found himself short of provisions, though what he lacked in meat he made up in liquor, which flowed without stint, I assure you. In this predicament, when he was told that so much good venison was passing his castle, he did not hesitate to sally out at the head of a band of his wild Highlanders, and seize upon it. The royal keepers remonstrated against this bold act, which they called " high treason," warning him that he and his clan would have to pay dearly for the stolen deer, — perhaps head for head.

But Buchanan laughed right saucily, saying, that if James Stuart was king in Scotland, *he* was king in Kippen, and, flinging the fattest buck over his shoulders, he strode into the Castle, followed by his men, bearing the remainder of the prey; while the royal keepers rode on to Stirling, with lightened horses, but hearts heavy with disappointment and chagrin.

Now, kings are quite as easily touched through their stomachs as through their sense of honor and dignity; —in this case, you see, James might justly consider him-self wronged and insulted in both ways. He was hot-tempered as well as fearless, so he instantly ordered his horse and set out alone to the castle of Buchanan. He arrived just as several huge haunches of his venison were set upon the table, and the feasting was about to recommence. He found a tall, broad-chested, long-bearded warder at the door, who, not recognizing the new guest, threateningly presented his battle-axe to him, saying gruffly that the high and mighty Laird of Arnpryor was at dinner, and must not be disturbed by such as he. But the king slyly slipped into his hand a piece of gold, — which somehow seemed to touch his heart at once, — and said, " Go up into the ban-queting-hall, my friend, and tell your master that the ***Guidman of Ballangeich*** has come to dine with the King of Kippen."

The warder grumbled a little, but went to the laird, and told him that there was a troublesome fellow at the door, with a red beard, who called himself " the Guid-man of Ballangeich," and insisted on coming in to dine with the King of Kippen.

When the bold Buchanan heard this, he turned pale, left the table in great haste, and running to the door, fell at the king's feet, and begged his pardon for making free with the royal venison, and sending such a saucy message to his sovereign. Now, much of the king's anger had evaporated in his gallop from Stirling; he was tired and hungry, he smelt the smoking hot ven-ison, and he heard within the hall the merry jingling of wine-cups and the pleasant laughter of ladies, — so, instead of taking the laird's head, which would have done him no good, or confiscating his lands, which he did not need, he very sensibly concluded to show mercy to his rash subject, — told him to get up from his knees, assured him that he had only meant to give him a little fright, that he had really ridden up from Stirling to dine with him in a neighborly way, and begged that he might have that pleasure, before the venison should get cold. So the two went in together, and the feast went on, without further interruption.

After this, the Laird of Arnpryor mended his manners, and was a faithful and humble subject, though he was a little apt to boast to strangers of-" His Majesty's visit to my poor castle." By the way, he never could get rid of the title of " King of Kippen."

At another time, when King James was out on one of his secret and solitary excursions, he was attacked by four or five ruffians, on the narrow bridge of Cramond. Being very strong and a good swordsman, he was able to defend himself for some time against all his enemies, but he received several slight wounds, and his strength was about failing him, when a peasant came running out of a barn near by, and seeing one man beset by such an unfair number, generously took his part. This peasant was armed only with a flail, but with that he boldly attacked the assailants, beat upon their heads and shoulders so sturdily, — in short, gave them such a sound thrashing, that they were soon glad to take to their heels. He then took the king into his barn, gave him water and a towel to wash the blood from his hands and face, and afterwards walked with him homeward to protect him from another attack.

Without letting out the secret of his own rank, the king asked his preserver who he was. The peasant answered that his name was John Howie-son,— that he was a poor bondsman on the farm of Braehead, which belonged to his Majesty. James then asked if there was any wish which he had particularly at heart.

" O yes !" replied John; " if I could own the farm I labor on, I should be the happiest man in the world, — happier even than the king, with all his riches and glory ; for it is n't likely that I would be bothered with so many cares, or beset" with so many enemies as he."

The king sighed at this, and honest John continued : " And now, if I may be so bold, please tell me who you are."

" O, I 'm the Guidman of Ballangeich, —just a poor man who has a small office in the king's palace; but if you will come to see me, next Sunday, I will try to recompense you for your assistance to-day, — at least I can show you the royal apartments."

John thanked him heartily, and so they parted.

The king did not fail to give orders that his country friend should be admitted, when he should ask at the palace-gate for " the Guidman of Ballangeich."

The peasant came at the time appointed, dressed in his "Sunday's best," and found the Guidman in the same disguise he had worn in his adventure on the bridge of Cramond.

James conducted his visitor through the state-apartments, and was not a little amused by his simple-hearted astonishment at their splendor and grandeur. At length he asked if he would like to get a peep at the king.

" By all means! — if I can do so without offending his Majesty," replied John.

" O, no fear of that," said James. " ' A *cat* may look at a king,' you know."

" But how shall I know his Grace from all the great nobles around him. Will he wear his crown ? "

" No, but he will wear a hat, or bonnet, — all the rest will be bareheaded."

He then led his friend into a great hall, filled with noblemen and officers of the court. John looked curiously about him for a moment, and then whispered : " Where is he ? —where is he ? I can't see him."

" Did n't I tell you," said James, " that you would know him by his hat?"

" I' faith then," exclaimed John, " it must be either you or I, — for they are all bareheaded but us two."

The king and courtiers laughed heartily at this; and when John Howieson left the palace, it was as the owner of the farm of Braehead, which he and his descendants were always to possess, on condition that the proprietor should be ever ready to present an ewer, basin of water, and a napkin for the king to wash his hands, whenever he should pass the bridge of Cramond, or visit Holyrood Palace. This form, in remembrance of the service done his king by John Howieson, was observed by him and his family down to the time of George the Fourth of England.

King James did not always show himself so kind and merciful as in these adventures. Though in general, and for those times, a just, wise, and generous monarch, he was in some cases very stern, stubborn, and revengeful. In his early youth he had been wronged and really oppressed by the Douglases, the most powerful, rapacious, and unruly family in Scotland, and from the time when he made his escape from them, and set up as an independent king, he devoted himself with all his energies to humbling and subduing these formidable enemies. It was a great, good work for the people; but it hardened his naturally kind heart, and in some instances left on his memory the reproach of injustice and cruelty. He seized upon the estates of all the Douglases, drove them out of the kingdom, and swore that he would never employ or show favor to any one of the hated name.

How well he kept his vow we shall see in the following story: —

# THE LITTLE DOUGLAS.

Among the banished Douglases, there was one who had been a great favorite with the King, for his generous and manly qualities, his personal strength, and skill in all warlike exercises. This was Archibald Douglas of Kilspindie. The king used to make much of him on all occasions of hunts and tournaments, and called him his " Greysteil," after a famous champion in a romance of that time. On his part, Archibald was devotedly attached to the king, and never lent his honest countenance to any plot against him. However, when his great family was disgraced, not even he was excepted, but sternly driven into exile with the rest,—King James, in his implacable hatred against the haughty race which for centuries had ruled, not only the Scottish people, but their sovereigns, being resolved to spare not even the friend for whom his own heart secretly pleaded. So Archibald of Kilspindie was obliged to seek a refuge in England, where he remained several years.

At length, getting to be aft old man, and pining to see his dear country once more, and the king whom, for all his harshness, he yet loved, he resolved to return to Scotland and make one last attempt to touch his sovereign's heart. He went to Stirling, and one day, when the king was returning from the chase, threw himself in his way. James knew him at a distance, and said, with a smile, " See, yonder is my brave Grey-steil! " But the next moment, he remembered his vow, and hardened his heart, and when he met his old servant, he pretended not to recognize him, but put spurs to his horse, and rode fast up a hill towards the castle. Poor old Archibald Douglas wore a heavy coat of mail under his clothes, but his heart so yearned for a reconciliation with his king, that he would not let him pass, but ran along by his side, and kept up with him, looking into his face now and then, with a wistful, re-proachful, heart-breaking expression.

But they soon reached the castle. James sprang- from his horse and hurried in, leaving the Douglas without a kind word or look; The old man sunk down at the gate exhausted, and faintly asked for a glass of wine. But the warder, knowing the king's -hatred for the whole kith and kin of the Douglases, gruffly refused him this charitable courtesy, and sent him away. King James afterwards reprimanded his servant for this inhospitable treatment, — but I don't see with what reason. " Like master, like man."

The king was the more angry at this attempt to soften his heart, for feeling con-scious that he had done wrong in resisting it; and the next day he sent word to old Archibald that he must prepare to go again into exile, this time to France.

After this cruel act, he went out: to amuse himself with hunting. He rode furi-ously all the afternoon, and said nothing pleasant to any one. Towards night, he got separated from his followers, and finally found himself lost in the deep forest, though in fact he was but a short distance from Stirling. In this strait, he was very glad to meet a boy, some eleven or twelve years old, who was picking his way on foot through a rocky glen.

" Hold, sirrah! " cried King James; " turn thee, and show me the way to Stirling Castle."

The lad paused, and looked up, showing 'a proud, handsome face, though it now wore a half-sorrowful, half-sullen expression.

" Thou speakest in a lordly style enough, Sir Huntsman," he replied; " an' thou wert the king himself, thou mightest be a little more courteous,— though, i' faith, 'tis hardly likely thou wouldst be. However, I will guide thee to a spot whence thou canst see the towers of Stirling: 'tis but a little way from here."

" Thanks, my brave lad. And now, wilt thou tell me who thou art ? Thou hast gentle blood, surely."

"I am called young Archie of Kilspindie, or the little Douglas," "answered the boy, proudly.

The king frowned as he rejoined: " Knowest thou not that *that* is a dangerous name to own in Scotland ? What dost thou here ? "

"I came from England with my grandfather, Archibald of Kilspindie, who came to solicit the king's grace, and is banished to France for his pains. I go with him."

King James liked the fearless frankness of the lad, and, smiling, asked: " Hast thou ever seen the king thou speakest of?"

"No, Sir Knight, nor care I to see him. I like him not."

"Why, prithee?"

" Because he is a churlish, unprincely fellow. When my grandfather, who had done him no harm, but good service, humbled himself to come in his way, he forgot that

'A king's face Should give grace,'

and made him—a brave old man, — *a Douglas!* — run beside his horse, as I run beside thine ; and, when he fainted at his gate, would not let his servants give him a cup of wine."

" Nay, nay, I — that is, he knew nothing of that!" exclaimed James. Then, after a moment, he added : " What wouldst thou say if I should tell thee that thou hadst been talking to the king himself ? "

Archie had already begun to suspect as much, but now he answered bravely, though with a deep blush: " I should say that his Majesty had heard honest truth for once. But, see! — there is thy castle. Farewell! "

" Stay," said James ; " I like thy spirit, albeit thy words are rather sharp and pert. Come with me to the castle for a little while; surely thou fearest not to go with thy king ? "

" No, sire," replied the little Douglas; " though I have heard say an ancestor of thine invited an ancestor of mine into that same castle, and then slew him with his own hands. I do not fear thee; thou art not treacherous, — thou art only somewhat cruel. I will go with thee."

When they arrived at the castle, the king led the way at once to the apartments of the queen, — the beautiful Mary of Guise, a French princess, — and presented Archie to her, saying : " See, I have brought your Grace a strange pet, — a saucy page, an unfledged eaglet, a lion's cub, — a young Douglas ! "

"A Douglas! — has not your Majesty vowed to show no favor to one of that name ? " said the queen, casting an admiring glance on the handsome boy.

"Ay, but *thou* hast not," replied James. "I give him to thee. He has done me a service, and I am willing that thou shouldst make much of him, for his own and his grandfather's sake. I loved Archibald of Kilspindie once."

"Wilt thou stay with me, my bonnie lad?" asked the queen, kindly laying her jewelled hand on the curly head of the boy.

Archie was softened to tears by her goodness, and his voice trembled as he answered: " I would fain stay with your Grace, — not for your royal state, but for your sweet face and gentle voice, —but I must go with my grandfather. I am all he has in the world."

" But," said the queen, " he is poor and old, and he must go away to Prance, which, though a brave, beautiful land, will seem strange and un-lovely to thee. Here at my court thou wouldst be at home,--thou shouldst receive a knightly training, shouldst have money and servants at thy command, and my kind favor to count upon. Wilt thou stay?"

" Alas, I cannot! — even if your Grace could make me prince of the realm. I could not forsake my grandfather," replied the little Douglas, with noble firmness. And he went out directly into the cold, dark night to seek him, — out into a cold, dreary world with him. He stayed beside him faithfully till the exile died, less of age and infirmities than with home-sickness and a broken heart, and young Archie was left alone in a strange land, poor and friendless, — yet happier than the King of Scotland, who soon after died of a fever, brought on by disappointment and remorse, in the very prime of his life.

# ROBERT BRUCE.

HAVE told you that within view from Stirling Castle is the memorable field of Bannockburn, — so called from the stream, or ***burn*** of Bannock, which runs through it. The great battle here fought, and the hero who here immortalized himself, had so much to do with the history and fate of Scotland, that I think I must go back a little, and briefly relate the story of This great patriot was born in 1274, probably at Turnbury Castle, Ayrshire, where he spent his boyhood. At the age of sixteen, he became Earl of Carrick, on the death of his mother.

In his early manhood, Bruce was not so noble a character as Wallace. Though by blood, one of the most prominent candidates for the Scottish throne, he, like his father and grandfather, lived mostly in England, at the court of Edward the First, the enemy and master of his country.

But the patriotism, sufferings, and heroic death of Wallace made a deep impression on him; he began to grow restless and remorseful, and at last an incident occurred which was the means of greatly changing his life and character. Like the other Scottish nobles who had taken the oath of allegiance to Edward, Bruce was actually in his service, and more than once, I am sorry to say, fought against his own countrymen, struggling valiantly for their freedom. After one of those unequal skirmishes, inglorious for the English, and doubly so for the traitor Scots who fought on their side, it happened that Bruce sat down to supper without washing his hands, which were somewhat stained with the blood that had dripped down from his battle-axe. This was observed by the nice English lords who sat near him, and they shrugged their shoulders, and whispered to one another, with sneers, "Look at that Scotsman, who is eating his own blood!"

These words reached, not only the ear, but the *heart* of Bruce, and filled him with horror and disgust, — not at the ungrateful English who, in spite of all his services, despised and hated him for a traitor, — but for his own unnatural and cowardly conduct. The blood upon his hands might truly be called his own, for it was that of his countrymen, his brothers, and should have been as dear to him as that which flowed in his own veins. So guilty and sorrowful did he feel, that, instead of resenting the words of the English lords as insults, he rose up meekly from the table, and, going to a chapel near by, he flung himself on his knees, and, weeping bitterly, prayed God to forigve him for his great sin. His sudden and humble repentance seems much like that of the Apostle Peter, for denying his Lord; and there was almost as much reason for it; for next to the crime of forsaking and disowning our Divine Master, is treason to our fellow-men.

Bruce did not stop at repentance, as too many do, but made a solemn vow to

God to try to atone for his past life, by doing all that he could to regain the lost liberties of his country. So he left the English court and army forever, and joined his poor countrymen, resolved to conquer or die with them.

At this time he was about thirty years of age, a tall, powerful, grand-looking man, who, like Wallace, excelled in feats of arms and gallant exploits. He was usually remarkably just and generous, but he had a quick and passionate temper, and was sometimes cruel and remorseless in his resentments.

In his claims to the Scottish crown, Robert Bruce had a rival in Sir John Comyn, called " the Red Comyn," to distinguish him from another of the family, who, from his dark complexion, was named " the Black Comyn;" and when he resolved to make a brave effort to drive the English back where they belonged, he thought he had better see this rival, and try to come to some amicable agreement with him about their mutual pretensions to power. So he requested an interview with Sir John Comyn, who met him in a church, before the high altar. During their talk, they unhappily came to high and abusive words. I *hope* the Red Comyn was the first to use them; and, finally, Bruce, getting greatly provoked, drew his dagger, and stabbed his rival. He then rushed out of the church, and called for his horse. Some fiiends, who were with him, seeing him look pale, asked what was the matter. " I am afraid I have killed the Red Comyn," he replied. " It will not do to leave such a matter in doubt," said one of them. " We will make it certain! " So they ran in and despatched the wounded man with their daggers.

I think this was the most cruel and dastardly deed ever committed by Robert Bruce. He had invited Sir John Comyn to meet him, as a friend, and at a place where the lives of all men were considered sacred, and where nothing should have tempted him to strike even his worst enemy. But, as through all his life he never ceased to grieve and suffer for that sinful and unmanly act, — as he spoke of it with tears on his death-bed, and as God and his murdered rival have doubtless forgiven him, long, long ago, I think we may as well try to judge him charitably; — at least, we '11 drop the matter here.

Bruce now publicly threw off all allegiance to the Sang of England, and, with a small army of devoted adherents, marched through the South of Scotland, took several fortified towns, and drove away the English invaders. His friends then insisted on his being crowned at Scone, the place where the Scots made their kings, in those days. There have been few men ever found great enough to decline kingly honors, when they could get a chance at them, — but in this case, it was really a brave and patriotic thing in Bruce to accept them, as they increased tenfold the perils of his position. Now, Edward had made off with the Scottish regalia some time before, — so a crown had to be manufactured for this occasion, — a plain, slender rim of gold, but it answered quite as well, and was as becoming to a rude soldier, as though it had dazzled the beholders with marvellous carbuncles, diamonds, and pearls.

The honor of crowning Scottish monarchs be-longed, by ancient right, to the family of Macduff, Earl of Fife. The Earl at that time was one of the renegade nobles in the service of Edward, and scornfully refused to perform his duty. But he had a sister who it seems was made of better stuff; — this was Isabella, Countess of Buchan, who, though married to another minion of the English, bravely declared for Bruce. Hearing of his present dilemma, she took possession of her husband's horses, and posted off to Scone, vowing that King Robert should be crowned by a Macduff, after all! She actually placed the crown on his head with her own fair hands,— and it answered just as well, and was doubtless quite as agreeable to the Bruce, as though her haughty brother, the Earl, or a venerable archbishop, with a beard a yard long, had performed the rite.

In the mean time, intelligence of the new rising under the new leader had reached old King Edward, in London, and thrown him into a terrible rage. He set about raising an army at once, and hurried it off to Scotland, under the command of Aymer de Vallance, Earl of Pembroke. Then-he sat down and wrote to the Pope, telling him all about the killing of the Red Comyn, — not dwelling on the murder, — that was a small, every-day affair, but on the sacrilege of shedding blood in so holy a place as a church, — and the Pope being duly horrified, laid upon Bruce the awful curse of excommunication.

Then King Edward set out himself with another army for the North,—vowing that he would never return till he had put down the rebellion and slaughtered all the rebels. But before he had reached the borders of Scotland, a mightier monarch called him hence, — and he went with as little delay as any common man.

When he found that he was really dying, he gave directions that his dead body should be boiled in a cauldron, till the flesh all came off of the bones, — and then that the bones should be sewed up in a bull's hide, and carried in front of the army, against his foes, the Scots. But Edward the Second thought best to disregard this strange last request of his father, and had him decently buried in Westminster Abbey, with this inscription on his tomb: *" Edward I., The Hammer of the Scotch ; "* — a very good epitaph, for he was always hammering away at that people, — knocking them down as fast as they got up. But they were rid of him at last, — even his poor old hones never went against them, and I doubt if they would have frightened them much if they had. It was only live Edwards they cared for.

Luckily for them, the new king was much inferior to the old, and after making a feeble attempt to carry out his father's plans, returned with his army to England.

Before this, however, Bruce had suffered severe defeats from the English under Pembroke. Disaster followed disaster, till he was driven with his family and adherents into the mountains, where they were exposed to great hardships and perils. He was even obliged at last to part from his queen, whom, with the Countess of Buchan and others of her ladies, he left under his brother Nigel's care, in the castle of Kildrummie, Aberdeenshire, while he and his men took refuge in the island of Rachin, off the coast of Ireland. Here he soon received the sad news that the castle of Kildrummie had been taken, his brother killed, and the queen with her ladies carried into captivity.

This was a very dark, discouraging time with Robert Bruce, and it is not strange that he felt almost ready to give up his brave undertaking. But, it is said, a slight incident renewed his resolution and decided his and Scotland's fate. One morning, as he was lying on his miserable couch, he noticed a spider trying to fix a web to a beam over his head. Three, four, five, six times he tried, and failed; and then Bruce remembered that he had fought just six battles against the English, without success, and he said to himself: " If the spider succeeds this seventh time, I'll take it as a lucky omen, and will try once more."

The spider *did* succeed, and Bruce took courage, never to lose it again.

I have always had full faith in this interesting little tradition, because I believe that God often influences the hearts of men in such unexpected ways and through such humble means, and because it teaches us that in his providence not even spiders are to be despised.

Soon after this incident, Robert Bruce returned to Scotland, to renew his struggle with the English, and his unworthy countrymen allied with them. I cannot begin to relate here all the adventures he met with, all the dangers he braved, all the hardships he endured, from that time to the battle of Bannockburn.

There are many thrilling stories in Scottish history told of him and his adherents, especially of his brave and faithful followers, James Douglas, familiarly called " the Good Lord James," — a beautiful title, which I hope he deserved,—and Sir Thomas Randolph, a nephew of Bruce's, and worthy of his blood. Some of the accounts of their prodigious exploits and hair-breadth escapes it really strains one's faith a little to believe ;but it is certain that they struggled long and bravely, and suffered much for freedom's dear sake, and that Bruce nobly redeemed himself from the reproach of his early life. He was beset by perils and foes,—wronged, hated, persecuted, outlawed, and hunted by bloodhounds, — but he kept up his heart and the hearts of his followers, — was always prompt and fearless in action, yet patient in waiting, trusting in God. And this, remember, was not for a few months alone, but weary years, as the great struggle he engaged in lasted somewhat longer than our Revolutionary war.

At length the decisive battle of Bannockburn was fought on the 24th of June, 1314. Bruce had chosen his position, and had time to prepare the field, by strewing a portion of it with sharp points of iron called **catthorps**, and by having pits dug, which were concealed by heather and brushwood, — a clever, though hardly fair plan for laming and entrapping the war-horses of the English. But King Edward's army was greatly superior to Brace's in number, and far better armed and equipped; so the Scots may be pardoned for resorting to some stratagems.

The English host came up with great pomp and parade, resolved to spare not a soul of all the rebel army, but to crush at once and forever the last hope of Scottish freedom.

The battle began in the morning, and soon became one of the most desperate and terrible engagements ever fought. Before rushing to the encounter, however, the Scots fell on their knees in prayer, imploring the aid of the Almighty arm in their cause. All Christian armies have chaplains, who pray against each other as soldiers fight; but, of course, nobody can suppose that God is ever on both sides.

For my part, I do not believe that He is ever present, helping one band or nation of his children to slaughter another; but I do believe that He always favors freedom and justice, by inspiring the hearts of patriots with a sense of right. Men are braver and stronger fighters for a good conscience; and it is better to go praying than cursing even into battle.

So, though the English fought well, and **seemed** much the stronger, they were beaten, and driven out of Scotland, which thenceforth belonged to the Scots.

True, other efforts were made, under both Edward the Second and Third, to re-conquer the country, but Bruce and his good generals were too strong for them; and finally the latter English king was glad to renounce all pretensions to the Scottish throne, and to give his sister Joanna in marriage to Robert Bruce's son David. True, after Brace's death, the Scots had a great deal of trouble and strife; but the fighting was among themselves, — a succession of family quarrels and civil brawls,—they had, at least, that comfort.

Robert Bruce reigned for several years, wisely and prosperously, and died peacefully, at his favorite residence on the banks of the Clyde, in his fifty-seventh year. In his last moments, he requested his beloved Douglas to have his heart embalmed, and to bear it to Jerusalem, — fighting his way, if necessary, through the hostile Saracens who held the Holy Land. The Good Douglas promised with many tears ; and when his royal master was dead, he collected a gallant train, and set out for Palestine, bearing the heart in a silver casket.

But, on his way, he stopped for a while in Spain, where it happened he found King Al-phonso at war with the Moors; and, thinking that Saracens were Saracens wherever they could be met with, he plunged into the fight, and was killed. His body was found lying over the silver casket containing the Brace's heart, as though he had thought of it last. This was carried back to Scotland, and buried under the high altar of Melrose Abbey,—which was as well for the heart, and no worse for the soul of the hero, which was, and is, safe in the keeping of God.

The character of Robert Bruce was by no means perfect; but his faults belonged mostly to his time,—his virtues were all his own. He had a bad early training,—he began life wrong; but he proved himself a true man at last, and left to his country not only a great fame, but a memory beloved and blessed forever.

In conclusion, I will relate a little incident, which I consider the most beautiful thing recorded of Robert Bruce. I have called him **Robert Bruce** all along, because I think that ample name sounds nobler than his formal title of "King Robert the First." Don't it strike you so ?

# THE IRISH MOTHER.

Not long after Robert Bruce had put down his enemies, and fixed himself firmly on the throne of Scotland, his brother, Edward Bruce, a gallant and courageous man, was invited by the Irish, who were in the midst of one of their countless rebellions against England, to come over and be their leader and king.

Robert, who loved his brave brother very dearly, not only gave him an army, but went himself to assist in the noble undertaking. The two Braces gained several battles at first; but the English forces, which were very strong, were led by excellent generals, and the Irish, who, it seems, never did know what was good for themselves, or who were their best friends, joined their old oppressors in great numbers, from jealousy of their new allies. So things took an unfortunate turn, and the little army of the Scots was obliged to give way and retreat before the multitude of their opponents. At last the generous Edward Bruce was killed, and his followers went home, wishing the Irish joy of the rulers they had preferred to him.

Some time before this, however, King Robert had been recalled to Scotland by pressing duties; but he went, fearing the worst, disappointed and sorrowful.

The incident which I promised to relate is this: —

One morning, when the Braces were about to commence a hasty retreat, before a large army of English and Irish, whom it would be imprudent to meet, and just as King Robert was about to mount his horse, he heard wild and piteous cries, which seemed to come from some woman in great distress.

" What is the matter ? " he asked of one of his guard.

" O, nothing, your Majesty, but a poor woman, a laundress, who has a new-born babe, and is not well enough to go on with us. She is crying with fear that she shall be killed by the enemy, and I do not doubt she will, if we leave her behind."

What was to be done ? They had no carriages or carts, and there was not time to construct a Utter to carry the poor woman and her baby. Most generals would not have given a second thought to them, knowing the great danger of a halt just then; but Robert Bruce, looking round on his men, said, with a generous glow on his cheek, and manly tears springing to his eyes: "Ah, fellow-soldiers, let it not be said that a man who has once himself been a helpless babe, and nursed by a mother's tenderness, should leave a woman and her infant at the mercy of barbarians. In the name of God, let the odds and the risk be what they may, I will fight, rather than leave these poor creatures behind me! So let the army draw up in line of battle, instead of retreating."

He was cheerfully obeyed by his officers and men,—for, thank Heaven! nothing is so catching as a genuine spirit of heroism and humanity,— but, to the surprise of all, their enemies sheered off, and refused to fight. Sir Edmond Butler, the English general, thought from Brace's halting and offering battle, that he had received a large reinforcement, and judged it not safe to hazard an engagement.

So the Scottish leader suffered no harm for his heroic delay; and yet, had the result been less fortunate, I do not believe he would ever have repented of that generous and merciful deed, which I am sure you will now agree with me is the best and kingliest act related of Robert Bruce.

Linlithgow,

# MARY QUEEN OF SCOTS.

ON our route from Stirling to Edinburgh, we had a view of the ancient palace of Linlithgow, once one of the noblest royal residences of Scotland. It stands high on the margin of a lovely lake, and, though in ruins, has still a great deal of architectural beauty and stateliness. Linlithgow was at first little more than a fort, built by Edward I., and afterwards occupied by his troops. It was taken by some of Robert Brace's men in the following clever and daring way.

The English garrison was supplied with hay by a farmer in the neighborhood, of the name of Binnock, who secretly favored Bruce. The Scots of old were famous for stratagems; and so, when one day the English governor peremptorily commanded this Binnock to furnish a large quantity of hay, the firmer laid a plan for making him pay rather more than the market price for that article. He concealed a large band of liberty-loving Scots near the gate of the fort, and charged them to be still, until they should hear the signal-cry, which was to be " Call all! call all!" Then he placed in the cart several strong, brave men, some half-dozen of whom were his own sous, — all well armed and lying on their breasts,—and these he covered completely with hay. The driver was a faithful, stout-hearted fellow, who carried in his hand a small axe, or hatchet. Binnock himself walked behind the cart, humming a merry tune. The warders, seeing only the farmers with the load of hay, which they expected, opened the gates and raised the portcullis, to let them into the courtyard. But as soon as they got well under the gateway, Binnock gave a sign to the driver, who instantly cut the oxen free from the cart and started them onward,—which of course left the cart standing right under the arch of the gateway. At this very moment, Binnock shouted out his signal, " Call all! call all!" and drawing a sword, which until then he had kept hid under his former's frock, he laid about him famously, like the vigorous, half-barbarous Scot he was. The armed men leaped up from under the hay and rushed upon the English guard, who tried in vain to close the gates, or drop the portcullis with that cumbersome ox-cart in the way. Then the men in ambush outside came pouring in, and the castle was soon taken, and all the English garrison killed, or taken prisoners.

Robert Bruce, when he became king, rewarded Binnock by the gift of a fine estate, which his family long enjoyed. I once visited at the house of one of the descendants of this patriotic farmer, Mr. Francis **Bennoch**, a Scottish gentleman, who, though living in England, still dearly loves his brave fatherland. I well remember how one day, when I happened to notice his armorial crest, — the device a cart and the figure of an ox, I think, — my friend told me this story of the taking of Linlithgow, in his own pleasant way.

The palace was at its highest point of splendor during the reigns of James IV. and V. and Mary Queen of Scots. This famous princess, the daughter of James V. and Mary of Guise, was born in an apartment on the western side of the palace, which is yet standing.

Doubtless many of you have read the story of this unhappy queen, but I trust none of you will be unwilling to refresh your memories with a brief review of her sad, eventful life here.

# STORY OF MARY STUART.

When James V. died, there was a great deal of scheming and quarrelling be-tween two rival parties for the regency, — for the privilege of wielding the supreme power during the long minority of his infant daughter. The two candidates were the queen-mother, and the Earl of Arran, the nearest male relative of the princess. So there were disputes, battles, and troubles of all sorts, before Mary of Guise, a clever and high-spirited woman, succeeded in placing herself in the chair of state, — about the most uncomfortable seat in the world. I cannot believe that the poor woman thought herself happy after all, surrounded as she was by enemies, and op-pressed by the great cares of government; but it is to be hoped that she felt she was in the way of her duty to her daughter and the country.

But happily all this time the pretty little Queen Mary knew nothing of these great political strifes and intrigues. Safe and quiet in her nursery at Linlithgow, she slept and ate, smiled and crowed, cut her teeth, and learned to walk and talk as care-free and happy as any peasant child in all her kingdom. Her dark time was not yet come.

When Mary Stuart was six years of age, she was sent to the French court, to be educated under the care of her mother's relatives. She was accompanied by four lit-tle ladies of rank about her own age, and all bearing her own name. These remained with her for many years, and were called " the Queen's Marys."

It must have been a pretty and touching sight to see the little queen and her lit-tle maids taking leave of their mammas, and setting sail for a far, strange land. How they must have cried and struggled and begged, titled ladies though they were, to go back on shore with those dear mammas ! What a dismal, damp, unsteady place the ship must have seemed to them, and how dark and deep and awful the sea must have looked to them, the poor little girls ! But their tears have all been wiped away, long, long ago, in the land where there is "no more sea," nor parting, nor grieving; — it is pleasant to think of that.

Mary Stuart soon became quite contented in her new home, and grew in beauty and accomplishments,— as did her Marys, though in an inferior degree, of course. They would almost have thought it disloyal to equal their mistress,— high treason to surpass her.

When Mary was about fifteen she married Francis, the Dauphin, who soon after became King of France. But not long did Mary enjoy the glory of being queen of two kingdoms; her husband, Francis II., died after a very brief reign, and finding herself neglected and unkindly treated at the court of his brother, Charles IX., and his mother, Catherine de Medicis, as thor-oughly wicked a woman as ever lived, she resolved to return to her own country, where she was now needed, — her brave mother having died of disappointments and very weariness, glad it seemed to rest, even in the grave, from the trouble and turmoil of her delegated sovereignty. When Mary left France she was just eighteen,— an elegant, accomplished, and clever princess, — graceful, winning, and marvellously beautiful, if we may trust the poets and historians of her time. I cannot describe her, as it has never been ex-actly settled, I believe, which of the many pictures of her yet in existence is the true one. If any of you ever visit the great palace of Ver-sailles, you may see as many as half a dozen different portraits of her, as different as can be; so you can have your choice. Some prefer one, some another.

Scotland seemed but a poor and dismal country to the young queen, coming from the rich, sunny land and gay court of France. Her Marys had loving mothers and kindred to welcome them home; but *her* mother was in the grave, and she had no kindred on whose love she could depend, no home but gloomy castles and for-mal palaces. Ah, what a glorious thing it is to be a queen !

The Scottish people, however, were very glad to get their legitimate sovereign back, — were proud of her grace and beauty, and rejoiced over her in their own rude, simple way. Sir Walter Scott relates, that, on the evening of her arrival at Holyrood Palace, no less than three hundred of the citizens of Edinburgh appeared under her window, and serenaded her all night long, " each doing his best on a three-stringed fiddle." This terrific serenade has not been set down by historians among poor Mary Stuart's great trials, but I doubt not she found it hard enough to bear at the time of it.

Queen Mary's misfortunes were of three different kinds, — religious, domestic, and political. Her first misfortune was in being a Catholic, when the larger number of her people were Protestants ; her second was in marrying a handsome simpleton; and her third grew out of these two. Her being a Papist was an enormous sin in the eyes of many of her Protestant subjects, which not all her loveliness, graciousness, and accomplishments could atone for. There was a celebrated Protestant preacher of that time, named John Knox, who used to thunder away at the court and queen, — sometimes rebuking her to her face in no very respectful terms, — little thinking, poor man! how full his own stern heart was of bigotry and intolerance. She may have deserved all he said; for she was fond of pleasure, and devotedly attached to her own church, for all its wickedness. I do not know but that, had she had the power, she would have burned heretics in her zeal, like her cousin, Mary of England, — though I doubt it much, for she was not naturally cruel; but I do not much doubt that Mr. Knox would have used gentler language in her presence, if she *had* had that power. As it was, his party was too strong to be put down, and he spoke his mind bravely, and made a clean breast of it.

The husband which Mary Stuart chose, principally for his beauty and showy accomplishments, was her kinsman, Henry Stuart, Lord Darnley. He was young, rash, self-willed, ambitious; and, with little sense and less heart, was a very poor husband for any woman, — and the proudest queen is, after all, a woman, with a heart to love and suffer. I think that Mary Stuart, with all her wit and spirit, would have regretted her foolish choice after a while, if her husband had been ever so good and faithful; but she might have made the best of it, and gone on loving him in a dull sort of a way, and been tolerably happy, as the world goes. But as it was, she not only tired of the spoiled, passionate, faithless young man, but grew to hating him bitterly. This is how it came about: She had in her suite, as private secretary, a handsome Italian youth, by the name of David Rizzio, who was a great favorite with her, and whom she treated with rather unqueenlike familiarity. Many of the courtiers were enraged at this, and hated Rizzio with a fierce, scornful hatred,—not for any crime of his,—not out of envy or jealousy,—O no! but because, forsooth, he was a foreigner, poor and low-born. But no jealous noble of them all hated as Darnley hated. He saw the society of the clever and agreeable Italian preferred to his by Mary, who no longer tried to conceal her contempt and dislike of her husband, and he vowed to destroy her favorite. Now this David, like David of old, was skilled in music, and Mary, like King Saul, loved to be soothed by his playing and singing, when she was vexed or sorrowful. But the time came when he sang no more sweet songs for her delight and consolation. One night, as he sat at supper with the queen and her ladies, in a small cabinet, Darnley and several other noblemen suddenly burst upon the merry little party, and murdered the Italian before the eyes of his mistress. Poor Rizzio clung to the dress of the queen, and implored her to save him, and she begged for his life with prayers and tears,— but all in vain! The conspirators dragged him through her bedchamber and the anteroom to the head of the stairs, where they despatched him with no less than fifty-six wounds. So the poor youth paid dearly for the queen's favor, and so it wag that the queen grew to hate her miserable husband.

Two months after this, Queen Mary gave birth to a little prince, who was afterwards James VI., and who inherited his father's heartlessness, his mother's irresoluteness, and the beauty of neither.

The next fevorite of Mary was a very different man from the gentle, song-singing Italian, — the Earl of Bothwell, a dark, stern, bloody-handed profligate. Again the virtuous courtiers were indignant,— again the preachers thundered away at her for her misplaced fondness ; for the wicked earl had a wife, and she had a husband of her own,—such as he was. It was this Bothwell who brought about the next domestic misfortune, or crime of the queen, — the murder of her husband. This took place at a religious house, called " Kirk of the Field," just beyond the city walls, where Darnley was lodged for a time, being ill with the small-pox. One dark winter night, the house in which he lay was blown up by gunpowder, deposited under his chamber by the hirelings of Bothwell. The earl himself was present, and saw the awful deed accomplished. Darnley was found in a neighboring field, not much disfigured, but dead, of course. So he paid dearly for being a king-consort.

It has always been a great question with historians whether Mary was, or was not accessory to the murder of her husband, and it remains a question which I do not think will ever be decided beyond all dispute. It is one of those secrets of human history which rest with God ; hut, as it is pleasanter to think well than ill of our fellow-beings, let us hope that she was wholly innocent of so dreadful a crime. We can safely do that.

The worst thing against Mary was her weak, suspicious conduct in regard to Bothwell, after the murder. She did not bring him to a fair trial, but continued to treat him with apparent favor. Perhaps she was afraid him, for he was very bold and powerful. But such cowardice is a crime in itself; and certain it is, that most of her subjects believed her not only weak, but wicked, and began to murmur against her, and declare that they would no longer be ruled by the profligate murderess; and when she suffered Bothwell to divorce his wife, and actually married him herself, the people broke out in open rebellion.

To her great mortification, Mary found that her army would not fight for her and her detested husband, but began to disband and go over to their foes. Bothwell, who, like all bullies and assassins, was cowardly and treacherous, forsook his wife, and ran away from the first battle,— ran till he got to the sea, where he took up the life of a pirate, a very proper career for him.

Queen Mary surrendered to the confederated Scottish lords, who took her in triumph to Edinburgh, where the people insulted her most grossly as she rode through the streets, accusing her of murder and all sorts of crimes, which conduct to a humbled and defenceless woman, however erring, does not speak very well for the humanity of the people, or the magnanimity of the victors who conducted her. But I am afraid that many who were most noisy in crying out against her in her hour of misfortune, would have fawned at her feet if she had still been in power, — even if she had made way with as many husbands as. Bluebeard did wives.

Queen Mary was then imprisoned in Lochleven Castle, cm a small island, where, with a few faithful attendants, she was strictly guarded by stern jailers, while her half-brother, the Earl of Murray, assumed the regency and the guardianship of the young Prince James. At Lochleven Castle, Mary spent nearly a year in sorrowful captivity, — walking sometimes in a little mouldy garden, embroidering with her maids, or looking out, from her lonely tower, across the lake, for deliverers that never came. At length, by her beauty, her smiles and tears, she so moved the kind heart of a young lad in the service of the Laird of Lochleven, one "William Douglas, that he got possession of the keys of the castle, and at night let out the queen and one of her maids, and rowed them to the shore, where several of Mary's friends, some of them powerful Catholic nobles, were awaiting her.

When William Douglas left the castle he locked the gates and flung the keys into the lake,— where, strange to say, they were found by a fish-erman, only a few years ago.

Queen Mary soon rallied a considerable army of adherents, which met the regent's forces at .Langside, and were defeated. Mary beheld the battle from a hill near by, and at its close, mounted her palfrey, her heart wild with grief and despair, and rode sixty miles before she stopped.

She took shelter in the Abbey of Dundrennan, where she made up her mind to seek refuge in England, and place herself under the protection of her cousin, Queen Elizabeth. This was the most fatal step in a life that was full of fatal steps. Queen Elizabeth hated her beautiful rival, and from the first treated her, not as an unfortunate sister sovereign, but as a captive and a criminal. For nineteen years she kept her a close prisoner, — only removing her from one gloomy castle to another more gloomy,—till at last she caused her to be tried for various crimes, and then, when the judges had pronounced her guilty, signed the warrant for her execution, — with a few strokes of the pen, condemned her to death. Mary Stuart was beheaded at Fotherin-gay on the 8th of February, 1587.

It takes but a little time and few words to say that Elizabeth imprisoned her cousin Mary nineteen years before beheading her,—but it was a long time for one woman to hold a deadly spite against another. It is an awful thing to think of!

"Wearily, lonesomely, sorrowfully must those long, dark years have passed to poor Mary Stuart, — so that when death came at last, even though armed with the headsman's axe, he was as welcome to her as was to the apostle the angel who delivered him from prison.

Mary died very heroically and like a Christian, forgiving and praying for her enemies. She left some faithful friends, who wept for her such tears as all the riches of the English queen could not purchase,— all her power could not wring from any human eye. She had also a pretty pet spaniel, who was greatly attached to her, and had to he taken by force from her bleeding body, — and now, through nearly three hundred years, the dumb grief of that poor little dog seems to plead with our hearts for his mistress.

Elizabeth Tudor lived without love, and so " without God in the world." Mary Stuart may have been as erring as that other beautiful Mary who poured precious ointment on the feet of our Lord Jesus, — but she also "loved much," and so we may hope was forgiven.

Edinburgh.

# LITTLE MARGERY AND HER KITTEN.

WE had but a few days to spend in the capital of Scotland, and, as ill-luck would have it, those few days were unpleasant. We happened there in the beginning of the wet season, early in October, and the sun scarcely shone upon us during our stay. He came out quite bravely once in a while, but seemed scared at the black, ugly clouds driving up against him, and went in directly. We were obliged to go about sight-seeing under a big, dripping umbrella, or trying desperately to peer through a drizzling " Scotch mist," which is a lazy, sullen sort of a rain; so you will not wonder if I seem to have rather a dim, uncertain recollection of the grand old town.

Edinburgh has a very beautiful and imposing site, "upon a cluster of eminences, at the distance of a mile and a half from the Firth of Forth," which you know is an arm of the sea. It is surrounded by a picturesque country, with noble wooded hills and flowery valleys, — plains and rivers and wild waterfalls, —parks, gardens, castles, and ivied ruins, — lovely and wonderful to see.

Upon the loftiest eminence stands Edinburgh Castle, on the site where, twelve hundred years ago, Edwin, a Northumbrian king, first built a fort, around which eventually sprung up a town, called, in his honor, Edwinsburgh, or Edinburgh. In the Celtic language, this town is still called **Dunedin**, or " the Hill of Edwin." In this way the king carved his name and founded his fame on a rock, though he was probably a rude, war-like prince, who could neither read nor write. The present castle is a very old building, and, from its position, so strong that it has never been taken by assault, though several times by siege, and once by surprise.

Randolph, Earl of Moray, — Brace's Randolph, — was one of the brave Scots who took it by surprise in a very bold and singular way. A Scottish gentleman by the name of Francis came to him in private, and told him that, when he was a young man, he lived in the castle, where his father was keeper, and that he knew a way of scaling the crags and wall, unknown to any other soul. It seems that his father, the keeper, had kept him a little too strictly, shutting him up within the dreary fortress, as though he had been a prisoner, or a criminal, till he rebelled, and, being a brave, adventurous fellow, contrived a plan of nightly escape to the pleasant town below. He made use of a small ladder for descending the wall, and then boldly slid, or swung himself down the face of the steep rock, where a slight misstep, or a moment's giddiness, might have cost him his life. He always returned before daylight, by the same way, clambering up the rocks, and scaling the wall; and he was careful to choose dark nights for his expeditions, as there was great danger of his being discovered by the sentinels. Yet he had gone and returned safely many times, for," to tell the honest truth," he said, "there was then a bonnie lassie living down in the Grassmarket, who was glad to see me when I came, and sorry to have me go." When the brave soldier said this, he blushed through his grizzly beard and the bronze of fifty summers; but his broad chest heaved with a great sigh when he added: " She was my wife afterwards; she is dead now, and it will be, I confess, a sad thing for me to climb again the steep path I used to leap down with so light a heart; yet, for my country's sake, I'll do it. I am ready to lead any who are brave enough to follow."

Randolph gladly accepted his offer, and one dark night, with a party of thirty picked men, undertook the ascent of the rock, led by Francis. They were obliged to scramble up the steepest portion of the way ; to swing them-selves from cliff to cliff, where the breaking of the least point of the rock, or the loosening of a stone, would have been a fatal accident. Their greatest danger was of being discovered by the watchmen of the fortress, as they could all have been destroyed by a few large stones rolled down the rock. While they were on their perilous way, and before they had reached the shelter of the wall, they heard the guard going its round, to see that all was well. The Scots crouched down against the dark rock, and the stoutest heart among them beat fast with anxiety ; but what was their dismay when a stone came rattling down upon them, and a sentinel shouted from the wall: " Aha! I see you well! " Of course they thought themselves discovered ; but as they could gain nothing but broken limbs and necks by a precipitate flight, they wisely concluded to lie down and keep still in the friendly darkness. And it proved that the soldier's cry was only a trick played upon his comrades, who, however, laughed and passed on, saying : " No, no, man ; you can't befool us with such silly false alarms. Your dirty Scots must be cats or foxes, to clamber up such rocks as those yonder." But they found out their own mistake, to their cost, a half-hour later, when Francis, Randolph, and 'their mon leaped over the wall, and killed or took captive the entire English garrison.

Edinburgh is divided into the Old Town and the New Town, which are so totally unlike as to seem like two different cities. The Old Town is that built within the limits of the ancient walls. For several centuries, citizens did not think it safe to live without these bounds, and, as the town grew in wealth and importance, it became very much crowded in population, and, being cramped for room, the buildings seemed to shoot up like trees in a thick forest, to a great height. They could afford room but for a single thoroughfare of any width, — High Street, extending from the Castle to Holyrood Palace, —the houses being divided by closes, or narrow alleys, so narrow, damp, and dark, that they looked like clefts in some bleak mountain's sides, in which cold, hideous shadows lurk day and night, driving back the light and warmth, — into which, it would seem, the cheery little sunbeams dare not drop, for fear of losing themselves and being forgotten, and not able to answer for themselves when the father-sun calls home his children at night.

These queer old monster houses look dismal enough now-a-days,— gray, and almost tottering with age, and nearly blind, with their narrow windows dim with dirt, and half-unglazed ; but they were more cheerful, as well as grander edifices, in their time. Each house was built to accommodate several families, — as many as there were stories, or *flats*, which ranged from five to ten or twelve, — all reached by a common staircase. It was more like a pile of houses, layer on layer, than a single building. The first floor was considered the most honorable ; after passing that, the higher you went in *flats*, the lower you sunk in gentility, till, strange to say, when you reached the attic, you were set down among the lower classes. Now, all the rich and titled and learned people have emigrated to modern houses in New Town, and there is not such a difference between families who inhabit those crazy, gigantic houses in Old Town; they are all dignified and dirty, ragged and respectable alike. The New Town lies to the northward of the Old, and is very neatly and elegantly built, — its handsome edifices looking all the more beautiful and comfortable in contrast with the grand but gloomy old piles which frown above, — many of them packed full of poverty and wretchedness.

Our first visit was to the Castle, from whose walls we should have enjoyed a wide, magnificent view, had it not been for that provoking mist. In the old palace of Queen Mary, a part of the Castle, we were shown the room in which King James the Sixth was born. It is very small, — scarcely more than a closet, and is only lighted by one little window, which opens directly on the dizzy, jagged precipice. This was a dismal asylum for the poor young queen in her sorrow, and a dark, prison-like place for the royal babe to open his eyes upon for the first time; yet I doubt if he minded it.

In another apartment is kept the Scottish regalia, which consists of a crown, a sceptre, a sword of state, and a treasurer's mace. These are splendid mementos of dead royalty. The crown sparkles and glows with many precious stones. It is not known how old this is, so we cannot tell how many royal brows have ached under it. Those costly stones really seem alive, — they twinkle and quiver so, — and yet they are cold, hard, unfeeling things, living on and on, and gayly sparkling, while their great and lovely wearers decay and die. Mary Stuart once wore that crown, and in her rich royal robes, with courtiers kneeling at her feet, and music swelling around her, and those brilliant gems making a glory about her head, she must have seemed more like a goddess than a mortal woman. Now, it is very sad to look on the red glow of those rubies, and on the keen flash of those diamonds, and think how soon the rose of life faded from her fair cheek, and the light went out in her beautiful eyes.

Prom the Castle, we walked down High Street, through the Canongate, — once the Court end of the town, but now one of its most dismal and dilapidated quarters, — to the Palace of Holyrood. On our way we stopped to see the old house of John Knox, Queen Mary's stern reprover. It is a quaint, brown edifice, moss-grown and mouldy. As you approach it, you see before you the rough old Reformer himself, in the act of preaching the very longest of his long sermons, — that is, a stone effigy of him, which seems to be haranguing the passers-by.

We also passed Moray House, the ancient town mansion of the earls of that name, and the Scottish head-quarters of Cromwell; and Queens-bury House, in old times the residence of the dukes of Queensbury, but in these days actually an almshouse. I wonder if the paupers are any happier for being in such an aristocratic asylum, and I wonder if they ever play at gentility among themselves, and make believe they are dukes and duchesses ?

Holyrood Palace was added to an Abbey by that name, founded by David the First. It was nearly all destroyed by Cromwell, but was rebuilt in the old style, by Charles the Second. Fortunately the portion of the palace spared was the northwestern angle, which contained the apartments of Queen Mary. We ascended to these by a stone staircase, very unlike the grand marble stairways of modern palaces, and came first to a vestibule, where the guide showed us some spots upon the floor, which he said in a solemn whisper were poor Rizzio's blood. We did not dispute him, but I am afraid we did not look quite as awestruck as he expected, for in that dark place it was extremely difficult to make out any spots at all in the floor, though some folks have seen them very plainly, and of quite a lively red, — *so they say*.

Next we were shown the queen's presence chamber, — a large, handsome apartment, out of which opens the queen's bedchamber, which is yet very much as Mary Stuart left it, except that the paintings are faded and the hangings decayed. It gives one a strange feeling to look upon the very bed on which she slept, and the silk counterpane that covered her, so many, many years ago. That old counterpane,— how often it must have been heaved up by the proud and indignant beatings of her passionate heart, or shaken by wild sobs, in lonely nights, when her sorrows came upon her! Then there was an ancient mirror which she had used, and 0, how I longed to have it show me, but for one instant, the beautiful face it had reflected a thousand times! This is a pleasant chamber, and though by no means very splendid, it is, to all readers of Scottish history, one of the most interesting apartments in the world. Opening out of it is the small cabinet, in which the queen, one or two of her ladies, and David Rizzio, once sat at supper,—the last supper of the poor Italian, when Darnley and the other assassins burst in upon them. The private staircase by which they ascended from the apartments of the king-consort was shown to us, — a dark, ugly passage,—just such a one as you would expect murderers to make use of, in stealing on their prey.

We afterwards walked through the picture gallery, where we were shown more than a hundred portraits of Scottish monarchs, which nobody believes in. It is said they were painted but a few years ago, for country visitors to gape at, and that a burly palace porter sat for many of them. I think it likely, for the daubs are quite fresh, and there is a strong family likeness running through them.

We visited also the beautiful ruins of the chapel in which Mary Stuart was married to Darnley, and where he was buried, after having been blown up by his enemies.

Back of Holyrood Palace lie the open grounds called "the queen's park," — the queen's pastures would be a truer name, as they are nearly destitute of trees. These include the height called Arthur's Seat, and Salisbury Crags,— which we did not visit, but advise you to, if you ever get a chance. We did ascend Calton Hill, however, — a noble eminence in the town, beautifully laid out with walks, and crowned with a monument to Lord Nelson, — a great idol, a sort of sea-god of the British nation, who, with the Duke of Wellington, is sculptured and painted, and pillared and carved, and busted and monu-mented, all over the three kingdoms. Near this shaft is what is called " The National Monument," — the beginning of a splendid temple in honor of the Scotsmen killed in the last war with Prance,— thirteen white marble pillars, which cost a thousand pounds apiece. The people's patriotism or purses gave out, and the temple will probably never be finished, but it will make a fine little ruin for travellers to admire, and learned men to dispute about a thousand years hence.

There is also on this hill a tasteful monument to the poet-ploughman, Robert Burns, whom the Scottish people do well to honor. But the chief pride and beauty of Edinburgh New Town, is the monument to Sir Walter Scott, a gothic tower, noble and imposing, yet very graceful and beautiful, like his great and wonderful genius, the glory of his native land, and the delight of the world.

I have not space here to touch upon half of the interesting sights and peculiarities of Edinburgh, nor to tell you how charmed I was (in spite of the weather) with that quaint, romantic, and most singular place ; but, in other chapters, I will tell you somewhat more. Though this dear old town does not contain such splendid cathedrals and palaces as many foreign cities can boast, I am happy to say that it has a great number of noble institutions, — palaces of learning, and hospitals for the sick and unfortunate, asylums for the old and destitute, — God's houses, if he has any on earth.

I do not mean to give you the history of any king, queen, or great personage whatever in this chapter, — I am merely going to amuse you with a simple, true little story, which I have laughed over more than once. I shall tell it in my own way, and if any of you think, from the title, it will be more foolish than profitable, why, just skip it.

In the good old days, when the Scottish people had a parliament of their own, and the Scottish nobility and gentry had not thought of forsaking Old Town, in one of those immense High Street houses which seemed to contain a little world in themselves, there lived an advocate by the name of Ramsay.

Now, the Ramsays were of very good family indeed, — they occupied the second flat, and looked down with some contempt, I fear, upon the occupants of the stories above them," whenever they met them on the wide common stairway, which went up and up, and dwindled off and off, like Jack's beanstalk, till it ended, not in a wicked giant's palace, but at the door of the topmost attic room, where lived a funny little dwarf, who made toys for good children. On the first flat lived Lord Glenalbin, a celebrated judge, to whom the advocate and his family looked up with great reverence, especially when they met him on the stairs, dressed in his flowing black robes and big white wig, on his way to court. Then there was something grand, almost awful, in his appearance, — in his solemn way of taking snuff, in his stern gait, every footstep falling although it decided the fate of some poor criminal. The Ramsays had two daughters, Phemie and Margery,—both very pretty, but very unlike. Phemie was a wild, mischievous girl, who dearly loved a frolic, and would not deny herself a joke, or a bit of sport, even if it must be at the expense of her best friend, or of a harmless, defenceless dumb creature. I never heartily like such children, though they sometimes amuse me. They don't wear well at home, — they are too like India sweetmeats, too spicy for every-day use, Very different was her younger sister, Margery, — a sweet, gentle, tender-hearted little girl, who loved fun well enough, but loved *love* better. Margery was her father's darling, but her mother, who was a tall, red-haired, mettlesome woman, liked Phemie best, for she said: " She is a lassie o' spirit, and no sic a saft, timorous, wee thing (not such a soft, timid, little thing) as the bairnie, Margery, — the Lord care for her, for she is one of his ain puir Meeting lammies!" (one of his own bleating lambkins).

Margery was very fond of pets. She had caged birds within doors, who sung their very sweetest for her, and tame pigeons without, who came daily to feed from her hands at the window; and, finally, her good father brought her home the dearest pet of all, — a pretty, gentle, playful kitten.

These were friends and playfellows for Margery, but Phemie only took delight in teasing them, and they in return feared and disliked her. The birds ruffled up their feathers and scolded at her from their cages, and even the meek young kitten, at sight of her, allowed an unbecoming anger to bristle in her whiskers, hump up her back, and swell out her taper little tail.

But we must return to Lord Glenalbin. It happened that the close which divided this house from its neighbor was very narrow,—not over six feet wide, and that across the way lived another lordship, a friend to the judge. On fine mornings, before going to Court or Parliament, these two noblemen often enjoyed what the Scotch call " a crack," that is, a chat, together, each leaning out of his chamber window.

One morning, when they were very earnestly engaged discussing some great political matter, the little girls, Phemia and Margery, were looking down upon them from the window above. Suddenly, Phemie ran away, but came back soon, laughing roguishly, and bringing Margery's kitten with a long silk cord tied about its middle, and in spite of the tearful entreaties of the little girl, who dared not openly resist any whim of her giddy and headstrong sister, she swung the poor scared creature over the window-seat, and let her down, down, and dropped her right on to his lordship's big white wig! Then, a little frightened at her trick, she began to pull in; but pussy, frantic with fright, fixed her sharp claws into the wig, and hung on desperately, so when she rose, the wig rose with her. Just imagine his lord-ship's surprise and horror, on feeling his wig lifted from his head, and seeing it go whirling up into the air, as though carried by invisible hobgoblins, — for at first he could not see the kitten and cord. But his friend over the way had seen the whole affair, and laughed uproariously at his ridiculous plight, — which did not help him take it good-humoredly. But his lordship was not, after all, very stern and haughty, though he felt it his duty, as a judge and a nobleman, to appear so, — and though justly shocked and indignant at the saucy trick that had been played upon him, when Mrs. Ramsay herself came hurrying down, all a-trem-ble with terror, and made a humble apology for her giddy-brained little girl, he was good enough to unbend and cool down, and to say, as he readjusted the wig on his noble head: " Weel, weel, my guid woman, dinna fash yoursel', — there 's na muckle harm done, — bairns will be bairns." (Well, well, my good woman,—don't trouble yourself, — there's not much harm done, — children will be children.)

When Mrs. Ramsay came back from this interview she rated her wild daughter soundly.

" What will you be aboot neixt ? — ye ne'er do weel! Can ye no turn your hand to something mair (more) respectable than dangling cats oot o' the window to catch honest men's wigs!—and will naething (nothing) content ye, but a *judge's* wig, a LAIRD'S wig, ye saucy hizzie ! As for the wee bit baudrons (the little cat), I'll tell ould Davie to gie her a toss into the loch, wi' a stane aboot her neck." (I '11 tell old David to give her a toss into the lake, with a stone about her neck.)

Poor Margery was filled with grief and horror at these words. She did not try to plead with her angry mother, but, folding her kitten close in her pinafore, she stole out of the room, ran down to the first floor, and asked the porter if she might see Lord Glenalbin. He was gone to the Parliament House. "Would you believe it, this timid little girl, brave now for her dear pet's sake, followed the judge even to that awful place ! The Court was not yet opened; and, without much difficulty, Margery found his Lordship, in the midst of a group of members of Parliament and advocates, amusing them with an account of his being so strangely unwigged that morning.

You see, he thought he would tell the story first, and laugh with the others, for he knew his friend would not keep such a good joke to himself. Little Margery crept up to his Lordship, and pulling at his long black robe, raising her soft, sad, appealing eyes to his face, and lifting up her kitten, who had just then given a piteous mew, she said: "Please, my laird, forgive my wee kitten, for lifting your lairdship's wig off your lairdship's head ! She did na ken (did not know) whose wig it was. Mither is sae sair fashed aboot it (is so troubled about it) that she says auld Davie shall drown my pet. Oh! will you no forgive the puir beastie, for I canna see her gang awa to dee!—it gars me greet to think o' it" (I cannot see her go away to die!—it makes me cry to think of it). And the poor child burst into tears.

"Hush, hush, my bonnie bairnie," said Lord Glenalbin, "they shall na kill your pet. Here, I'll write her pardon; tak' it to your mither, and, I 'll answer for it, she will na harm a single hair o' the wee baudron's head. But mind, lassie, ye must na do it again, — you are ower young (too young) to angle for big wigs."

Margery did not tell him that she was not the saucy angler, — she thought that would not be generous to her sister; she took the paper, humbly thanked his Lord-ship, and ran home.

When Mrs. Ramsay read the lines her little daughter brought from Lord Gle-nalbin, she not only forgave pussy, but took her into great favor, though she never could abide cats before. She continued to befriend her, and nursed her in her old age, — for she considered that cat as having been the mating of her family, by bringing them into some connection with the nobility. And so she *had*, for Lord Glenalbin took a great fancy to his little petitioner, Margery, which lasted all his life; and I have either heard, or dreamed, that his noble young son, who inherited his title and estates, inherited this fancy also, and that Margery finally became Lady Glenalbin, and made one of the prettiest Ladyships in all Scotland.

Edinburgh.

# THE MARQUIS OF MONTROSE.

THE principal religious edifice of Edinburgh is the Ca-thedral of St Giles, founded some time in the fourteenth century, and named after the patron saint of this town; for it is a Catholic belief that saints not only act as guardians and media-tors for individuals, but often take whole cities and coun-tries under their protec-tion.

St. Giles's Cathedral, or the High Church, as it is now called, is not a very beautiful building, but it has a venerable look, and has many interesting historical associations. It was here that James the Sixth took leave of his Scottish subjects, as he was about to proceed to England, to succeed Elizabeth; and it is recorded that the people actually *" wept"* at losing him. But in St. Giles's Cathedral occurred a yet more important event than this royal farewell. Here, on the 13th of October, 1643, was sworn to and subscribed by the Committee of Estates in Parliament, the Commission of the Church, and the English Commission, *the Solemn League and Covenant* between the English Puritans and the Scottish Presbyterians. Another league, called the *National Covenant*, had six years before been adopted by the Scottish people alone, as a defence against the encroachments of Prelacy, or Epis-copacy. Now, in this chapter, and the one which will follow, I shall try to give you a clear, though brief account of these Covenants and the Covenanters, as no one can have a good idea of the history of Scotland without fully understanding the religious questions about which the people and their rulers differed so long and bitterly. You will not find this account amusing, but I hope I know you too well, dear children, to fear that you will turn away dissatisfied from the serious records of history, or the plain words of instruction. The reformation in Scotland was much more thorough and hearty than in England. Some of the reformers were too stern, hard, and uncharitable ; but they had a stern, hard work to do, and so much perse-cution to endure, that it is little wonder they could not keep themselves in a very amiable frame of mind. Most of them were honest and earnest men, who had the good of their country and the glory of God at heart. The forms and titles of the English Church were not very different from those of the Church of Rome, though the king was declared its head, instead of the Pope. But the Kirk of Scotland was as opposite as possible to the Church of Rome, in its forms and government. The Presbyterian system was simple and strictly republican. The affairs of the kirk were administered by representatives, meeting in assemblies, and elected by votes, and no great head of the Church was acknowledged, except Christ himself. The Scottish people went out in a great body from the Church of Rome, because their conscienc-es condemned its corrup-tions, and their proud spirits rebelled against its tyranny. The English people were mostly ***driven*** out, by their hot-headed king, Henry the Eighth, who had taken a spite against the Pope; and fox many years they secretly longed to get back, and clung for dear life to as many of the Romish forms and ceremonies as their Pope-kings would allow them. So it could hardly be expected that there would be much sympathy between the Eng-lish and Scotch Protestants, though there was really very little difference between the doctrines they professed. King James the Sixth, who was never more than half a man, showed no affection or gratitude toward the Protestant clergy, through whose power he had been placed on his poor mother's throne. The stern old Presbyterian preachers were little to his taste. They refused to flatter him, but bolted out their disagreeable truths, and thundered forth their rough reproofs and admonitions to his face. On one occasion, when an uncommonly free-spoken divine was preaching before him, the storm of pious rebuke came so hot and heavy that the king, jumping to his feet, called out, angrily: " Speak sense, mon, or come down fra the pulpit!"

The minister grew very red in the face, but answered, with becoming spirit: " I tell thee, mon, I will neither speak sense nor come down fra the pulpit." When, in 1603, James was called to the English throne, be determined to unite the religions as well as the governments of the two nations; and disliking Presbyterianism, he resolved that it should be made to yield to Episcopacy, and that Scotland should "conform" to England. His first tyrannical act was to punish by banishment, and in other ways, six clergymen, for holding a general assembly without his leave. He next caused measures to be passed by the Parliament at Perth, restoring the order of Bishops, which the Bark had abolished. Then, by threats and bribery, he effected the passage of laws introducing the rites and ceremonies of the English Service into the Scottish Church. The day when Parliament ratified these new laws, called ***the Five Articles of Perth***, was long after spoken of as " the black Saturday." Alas! Scot-land had many such black days! The larger part of the clergy and laity refused to accept the new forms of worship, and were cruelly punished for nonconformity.

In 1625 James the Sixth died, and was succeeded by his son, Charles the First, who, you will recollect, was put to death by Cromwell and his party, in 1649. He had some amiable, manly qualities, — he was a good husband and father, which is more than could be said of many of the Stuart family,—but he was not a good king, and he has been pitied more than he deserved, I think, — chiefly because he was an elegant, accomplished prince, — dignified, melancholy, handsome, and wore his hair in long, glossy curls over his shoulders. It is very hard to lose one's head, even if it has never been anointed and worn a crown; but Charles put his to no good use, and by his foolish acts seemed bent upon getting rid of it. He was rash, obstinate, unreliable, and despotic. One of his most foolish and fatal undertakings was to carry out his father's plan of making the Scots conform to Episcopacy. He ordered his English bishops to prepare a Liturgy, or Book of Common Prayer, for the Scottish Church, and sent down his most royal commands that it should be universally adopted by the clergy and people.

Sunday, July 23d, 1637, was the day appointed for the introduction of the new service-book into the churches of Edinburgh. A multitude of people, including all the great lords and magistrates of the city, assembled at the High Church of St. Giles. The Dean of Edinburgh was to officiate, and at the time set for the service, he came out of the vestry, dressed in his surplice, and trying to look solemn and priest-like, but evidently feeling not a little nervous and awkward. He passed to the reading-desk, and began reading the service, in a loud, but rather unsteady voice, while the people looked on silently,—some curious and wondering, as though at a show, but the greater part sullen wid indignant. Among those who showed most horror and anger was an old woman by the name of Jenny Geddes. She was not learned, nor great,—she was only the keeper of a green-grocer's stall in High Street,—but she was a dame of spirit, and a stanch Presbyterian, who hated Episcopacy next to Romanism, and Romanism next to the Evil One himself. This morning she sat on a little stool, near the desk, — but sat very uneasily from the first,—boiling over with indignation. When the Dean came out in his robes, she tossed her nose in the air with disgust, and muttered something about "Popish rags." Then she drummed impatiently with her foot, fidgeted, and frowned, and took snuff, and glowered at him with her twinkling black eyes. At length, when he came to announce the " Collect" for the day, it seemed she could con-tain herself no longer, but springing to her feet, she caught up her stool and flung it at the poor Dean's head, calling out at the top of her shrill voice: " Deil colick the wame o' thee, thou fause thief! dost thou say the mass at my lug ? " which, translated into plain English, means, I ana sorry to say, something very like this: " The Evil One give thee the colic, thou false thief! dost thou dare to say the mass in my ears ? " A very unkind and impolite wish, certainly; but those were rude times you know, and Dame Janet was very much excited. The throwing of her stool was the signal for a general uproar. All the women of the congregation rushed towards the desk, threatening to tear the surplice from the Dean's shoulders ; but he very prudently slipped it off, and while they were ripping and rending it to pieces, made his escape, and ran like a frightened hare till he reached his covert, the Deanery.

Then the Bishop of Edinburgh mounted the pulpit to call the people to order; but he soon dismounted, for he was not only saluted by cries of " a Pope! a Pope ! " and other hard names, but by a regular storm of stools, and even stones! for the men, grown as courageous and excited as the women, were all up in arms, and chose rather to fight than to pray in the new way.

This riot was the beginning of a stout and universal resistance to the introduction of the service-book. The king was as obstinate as his subjects, and sent commands to the magistrates to punish the rioters severely, and enforce the reading of the Liturgy. Then the people banded together, and drew up and signed the great **National Covenant**, by which they bound themselves to oppose Episcopacy and defend Presbyterianism with their lives. Hundreds of thousands eagerly signed this covenant, though they knew it might expose them to persecution, and even to martyrdom. Some signed it with one hand raised to heaven and tears streaming down their cheeks, — and some drew blood from their arms and dipped their pens in it, to make their oaths more solemn. Such a people as this were a match for any tyrant, as Bang Charles found to his cost. After declaring war against his rebellious Scottish subjects, and fighting several battles with the Covenanters, he was obliged to abandon his purpose, and make to them some important concessions. It was to a Scottish army that he finally surrendered himself, and, I regret to say, it was a Scottish army that sold him to the English Parliament.

When Charles the First was put to death, the Parliament of Scotland resolved to support his son, Charles the Second, provided he would sign the Covenant. This he did, though he hated Presbyterianism even more than his father and grandfather had done. He said it was not " the religion for a gentleman," — a singular objection for a prince to make, who, it seemed, did not think any folly or vice ungentlemanly.

Charles signed the Covenant for nothing; his Scottish army was not strong enough to contend with the English forces, and he was obliged to retire to the Continent, and there remain till after the death of the great Protector, Cromwell. That old lion out of the way, he came back to England, and ascended the throne; and the people rejoiced as though this had been a happy event, and not, what it proved, a heavy misfortune.

One of the most marked men of the time of which I have written was the Marquis of Montrose, of whose eventful history I will give you a brief sketch.

# THE STORY OF MONTROSE.

In the more prosperous part of the reign of the first Charles, there appeared at his court a young nobleman, who eclipsed all the courtiers in graceful accomplishments, all the wits in ge-nius, all the scholars in learning, and the king himself in beauty and dignity. This was the Marquis of Montrose, a brave soldier, and, what is better, a noble poet. He not only wrote poetry himself, but has been the innocent cause of a great deal of poetry in others, for there was much that was splendid in his character and romantic in his career. He had a rash, fiery spirit; he was too ambitious, and sometimes too unscrupulous and unforgiving ; but he was never mean or cruel, and never sought to advance himself by false, underhanded means.

The young Marquis was not favored or distinguished by King Charles as he felt that he deserved to be, and, in his proud resentment, retired to Scotland and declared for the Covenant. It was a great pity that he was not actuated by *principle*, instead of pique, in taking this step. However, the Covenanters received him with open arms, and the king soon had cause to repent having turned the cold shoulder to him. The Lords of the Covenant employed him in several important undertakings. At the battle of Newburn, he performed a very gallant exploit. He forded the Tyne alone, under a hot fire of the English, to ascertain the depth of the water, before leading over his regiment.

But, for all his brave deeds and valuable services, the Lords of the Covenant were envious or stupid enough to slight him, and advance above him the Duke of Argyle, a cunning, crafty man, who pretended great devotion to his country, but in his close, dark heart was selfish, scheming, and revengeful.

The families of Argyle and Montrose had been at enmity for centuries. The present Duke was the personal foe of the Marquis; so Montrose was doubly angered and mortified at his being preferred to him. He grew sullen and dissatisfied. He had never really liked Presbyterianism: it was too strict and solemn for him, a gay young nobleman, who loved pomp and pleasure, and magnificent dress ; and now he felt only contempt and aversion for both Covenant and Covenanters. In this state of mind, the king had little trouble in winning him over to the royal cause, to which he ever after remained faithful. He became the leader of the Scottish cavaliers, the most popular, gallant, and splendid of them all. He suffered some severe defeats at first; but he kept up his great heart and persevered, till finally the praise and the fear of him filled the kingdom. He took town after town, and won battle after battle. The king sent him a commission, naming him Captain-General and Lieutenant-Governor of Scotland; then, just as he was flushed with the generous hope of being able to march into England and put down all King Charles's enemies there, his reverses came upon him. He lost the battle of Philiphaugh, upon the borders, and was obliged to retreat to the Highlands, when so many of his followers basely deserted him that the king commanded him to save himself by leaving the kingdom He reluctantly obeyed, and in disguise escaped to Norway. He remained abroad until after the beheading of the king, when he transferred his allegiance to Charles the Second, and, with a small army of Germans and Scotch exiles, landed in Scotland, to strike for the rights of the prince. It was a rash enterprise, and speedily failed.

In their first engagement with their powerful enemies, the royalists were defeased, and Montrose himself was obliged to assume a mean disguise to make his escape. He wandered about till he was exhausted by hunger and fatigue, when he allowed himself to be taken prisoner by a Scotch laird, one MacLeod, — feeling sure, in his noble, unsuspecting heart, of protection, as MacLeod had once been a follower of his. If any of that man's blood ran in my veins, I should blush to own the truth, that he delivered up his old friend and chief for a miserable reward.

The Covenanter leaders were mean enough to treat their unfortunate captive with cruelty and insult. They took him from town to town, exhibiting him in his humble disguise, — mocking him and railing at him. The people of the town of Dundee alone, though they had once suffered severely from the excesses of his troops, showed themselves forgiving and magnanimous. They supplied him with money and clothing suited to his rank, and refused to treat him like a common criminal.

Before Montrose reached Edinburgh, he had been condemned to death, as a traitor, by the Parliament, without a trial. He was sentenced to be hanged by the common hangman, on a gibbet thirty feet high,—his head to be placed on the Tolbooth (the prison), his body to be quartered, and placed on the gates of the principal towns of Scotland. By the order of that same vindictive Parliament, he was met at the gates by the hangman, dressed for the time in the Montrose livery, and conducted to jail on a cart, bound and bareheaded. It was expected that he would be overcome by this humiliation and the insults of the populace ; but he bore himself so grandly, and looked about him with such noble dignity and calmness, that the rude rabble, instead of jeering, were awed into silence or moved to tears. When he appeared before Parliament to hear his sentence, he conducted himself in the same calm, heroic way, and defended himself with great eloquence.

In reply to the Chancellor's charge of breaking the Covenants, he said he had indeed taken the *National Covenant*, and stood by it, until it was used more in assailing the royal rights of the king than in defending the religious rights of the people; but as for *The Solemn League and Covenant*, he had never signed it, and was not bound by it.

When his hard sentence was read to him, he did not flinch, but remarked that he would be more honored by having his head placed on the Tolbooth than his portrait in the king's bed-chamber; and as tot his body being quartered, he wished he had flesh enough to send some to every city of Europe, to testify of the cause for which he died.

That night he wrote a poem, expressing these same heroic sentiments. 0, the pity of it, that the king and the king's father were so utterly undeserving of the devoted loyalty, the noble blood, of such a man as Montrose! But never a Stuart of them all was worthy of such a sacrifice.

The Presbyterian clergy labored with the Marquis to obtain from him a confession of political crimes. He meekly acknowledged that, ***as a man***, he had many sins to repent of; but he declared that towards his country and his king he had " a conscience void of offence."

One Johnstone, a famous Covenanter preacher, intruded upon him as he was dressing, the day before his execution. Seeing the prisoner combing and curling his long, beautiful hair, Johnstone gruffly remarked that he might be more profitably engaged at so solemn a time.

" May it please you," replied the Marquis, with a haughty smile, " I will arrange my head as I fancy, to-day, for it is still my own; to-morrow it will be yours, and you can do with it as you please."

Montrose walked from the prison to the place. of execution in the Grassmarket, where the terrible gibbet stood black and high. Here the Pres-byterian preachers came about him again, like a flock of ravens, prophesying misery and wrath, if he died without acknowledging his guilt. He answered them gently, but turned from them to the hangman, as though he had been a friend. As a last insult, a book containing a history of his life was hung about his neck by the executioner; but again

Montrose defeated the spite of his enemies, by saying that he felt as much honored by such a record of brave deeds and loyal services as he had been by the badge of the Order of the Garter, which the king had bestowed upon him. At last he submitted himself to the hangman so calmly, and died so courageously, that a great shudder ran through the crowd, and sobs and groans arose on the air; and when some of his bitter enemies looked up and saw his noble form slowly swinging above them, they felt that it would always be between them and heaven, and must bar them away from God forever.

This sad execution happened on the 21st of May, 1650. Some writers say that Argyle exulted over the death of his rival, and others, that he was shocked by it, even to tears. Now, though I do not admire the character of the duke, I prefer to believe that the latter account is the true one.

Edinburgh.

# THE TWO MARGARETS.

THE Presbyterians of Scotland had very little confidence in Charles the Second, though he had signed the Covenants with the utmost solemnity. So they sent one of their number to London, to attend the meetings held there to arrange for the recall of the king, to stand up for the interests of Presbyterianism. This was a Mr. James Sharp, a minister in the Presbytery of St. Andrews, who in the end proved too sharp for his employers altogether, — for when he reached London, and found which way the wind blew at court (decidedly in favor of Episcopacy), he made a secret agreement with Charles to do all in his power to forward the royal plans, provided he could receive the Archbishopric of St. Andrews and the Primacy of Scotland.

Two other traitors to the Covenant, and tools of the king, were the Earls of Middleton and Lauderdale, — one the Royal Commissioner in Parliament, the other the Secretary of State, and both hard, coarse, unprincipled men. One of their boldest proceedings was to call a parliament and pass acts doing away with all the laws passed during the preceding twenty-two years, declaring the Covenants illegal, and prohibiting their renewal. These tyrannical enact-ments were not passed without threats and bribery, and only, it is said, after "a drunken bout," — a shameful way of legislating, which unfortunately has not quite gone out of fashion. We Americans need not go back two hundred years, into the history of a foreign country, to know that such things have been.

The people were greatly outraged by these high-handed proceedings, but did not rise in revolt till they were driven to it by actual persecution. Middleton and Lauderdale singled out several prominent Presbyterians, and brought them to the scaffold. Among these were the Marquis of Argyle, a minister by the name of Guth-rie, and a Captain Govan. Guthrie suffered for writing a book against the course of the king, and Govan for having brought the tidings of Charles the First's execution to Edinburgh, and spoken of it as " good news." I am sorry to say that there is little, if any, more liberty to print or speak unpleasant truths, in several of the kingdoms of Europe, at this day.

The Argyle they executed was the old enemy of Montrose. His bleeding head now replaced on the Tolbooth that of the Marquis, whose almost fleshless skull and limbs were brought together and buried, with immense pomp, in the Cathedral of St. Giles. And so matters went, in those dreadful times, — heads up, and heads down, like a horrible game of see-saw: heads on, heads off—but, unhappily, never on again.

Middleton, Lauderdale, and their crew next passed an act for ejecting from their parishes all clergymen who would not conform to Episcopacy. This, also, was one of " the drunken acts" of the depraved king's councillors. To their immortal honor, hundreds of clergymen refused to conform to a church government which their consciences could not accept, and were deprived at once of their means of liv-ing, and, with their families, driven from their homes, and thrown upon the chari-ties of a poor and distracted country.

They were succeeded by a miserable set of curates, — for the most part ignorant and unprincipled men, — whose bad hearts despised the holy Word of God they dared to utter, and whose dissolute lives were a blasphemy against Him they professed to serve. It was little wonder that the moral and devout people of Scotland refused to attend upon religious services administered by such men. Some were weak and worldly enough to conform; but by far the greater part, of the peasantry at least, stood bravely by the Covenants. They followed their banished ministers to their retreats among the hills, and would have none others to instruct and guide them. Everywhere they held secret meetings for preaching and prayer, — but especially in the south and west of the kingdom. They met in private houses, in barns, or in the open air. These unlawful assemblies were called **Conventicles** and **Field-meetings**. Lauderdale and company took severe measures to punish the **Non-conformists**, and compel them to attend upon the services of the curates. They passed another act, commanding all the Covenanter ministers to remove twenty miles from their parishes, and forbidding them, on pain of death, ever to come within that distance of their old homes. They posted troops throughout the districts where there was most of the Covenanter spirit, to awe and oppress the people, and drive them to church, as sheep are driven into a pen. These lawless soldiers committed all sorts of outrages upon the common people, while their ferocious leaders took in hand the Presbyterians of better condition. They robbed and destroyed, — they fined and imprisoned, — and, too often, shot down their unarmed victims without legal arrest or trial. But no injustice or cruelty could daunt or subdue the fearless and faithful Covenanters. Meeting after meeting was violently broken up ; yet still they were held in the shadowy glens and on the heathery hills, and more and more numerously attended. Sir Walter Scott describes one of these, and I will quote his fine description, to give you an idea of the singular and impressive scene presented at such gatherings.

" The meeting in question was held on the Eildon Hills, in the hollow betwixt two of the three conical tops which form the crest of the mountain. Trusty sentinels were placed on advanced posts all around, so as to command a view of the country below, and give the earliest notice of the approach of any unfriendly party. The clergyman occupied an elevated temporary pulpit, with his back to the wind. There were few or no gentlemen of property or quality,— for such persons could not escape detection, and were liable to ruin from the consequences. But many women of good condition, and holding the rank of ladies, ventured to attend the for-bidden meeting, and were allowed to sit in front of the assembly. Their side-saddles were placed on the ground, to serve for seats; and their horses were *tethered* in the rear of the congregation. Before the females, and in the space between them and the pulpit, the arms of the men present — pikes, swords, and muskets — were regularly piled in such order as is used by soldiers, so that each man might, in an instant, assume his own weapons."

Sometimes those weapons had to be used. A sentinel would give the alarm, and a troop of dragoons or a regiment of foot-soldiers would come dashing down from the hills, or stealing up from the glens, to attack the worshippers. Then the Covenanters, with the minister at their head, would grasp their arms, and fight manfully for the protection of their wives, mothers, sisters, and children. Sometimes there were terrible scenes of cruelty and slaughter, and the rocks of the mountain or the flowers of the glen were reddened with the blood of the martyrs.

But, when all went peacefully, how strengthening and comforting it must have been for those poor persecuted ones to meet thus,—to listen to a beloved pastor's voice, and pray and sing together. And how grand their solemn psalms must have sounded, pealing up among the hills, and echoing from peak to peak! — and how sweet their hymns, swelling on the fitful breeze, mingled with the songs of birds and the murmur of distant waterfalls ! What a sublime place to worship God in ! — mightier and more beautiful than any temple ever built by men.

Perhaps the good, earnest-hearted Covenanters often imagined that God's angels were listening to their voices, — standing but a little way above them, — veiled from their sight by the mists of the mountain-tops. And doubtless they were.

In 1666 the Covenanters had an unsuccessful revolt, called " The Pentland Rising." Many of those engaged in this were captured, and put to death, — some with frightful tortures. They all died nobly.

The chief military leaders of the persecuting party were Sir James Turner, General Dalziel, and John Graham of Claverhouse. These three remorseless men have been execrated and despised ever. since, — and they deserve all the blame and shame they have received; yet they were not so guilty as the statesmen and prelates who urged them on to such horrible excesses of barbarity.

At length the persecutors themselves grew weary,— even the king expressed himself "shocked " by the accounts from Scotland; so for a while milder measures were adopted. But the stern old Covenanters could no more be coaxed than driven into conformity, — they stood out as stoutly as ever; and their persecutors, when they had taken a little breath, began again, more furi-ous and ferocious than before. They raked up some barbarous old laws, long out of use, and brought them to bear against the Covenanters. The king (the same who had been so shocked) published what were called " Letters of Inter-communing," by which " his majesty command-ed all his dutiful subjects not to intercommune with any of the rebels, nor furnish them with meat, drink, house, or harbor, nor to have any intelligence with any of them by word, writ, or message, under pain of being considered guilty of the same crimes as the persons intercommuned."

By this cruel command more than 17,000 persons were made homeless outlaws, reduced to dreadful privations, and many suffered death. Another wicked measure of the persecutors was to invite several thousand wild Highlanders to ravage and plunder the Lowlands, where the Covenanters were the strongest. I am sorry to say that the mountaineers performed their task mercilessly, — stripping whole prov-inces of everything valuable which could be carried away.

In 1679, the traitor, Archbishop Sharpe, was assassinated by John Balfour of Burley, who wrongly imagined he was doing God's service; and shortly after Claverhouse was defeated at the battle of Drumclog. The Covenanters took cour-age, and raised an army of six or seven thousand men. The king sent against them a greater force, commanded by the Duke of Monmouth, and attacked them by Both-well Bridge, on the River Clyde. The Covenanters might have been victorious, if they had been prepared and united among themselves. But they had been indulging in violent political and theological discussions for more than a fortnight, and were so exhausted, out of temper, and out of heart, that they could not stand against the enemy. They were defeated, and left four hundred of their best men on the field. Bothwell Bridge was piled with the fallen, so that when Claverhouse charged across it, his terrible black war-horse went plunging and leaping over great heaps of the dying and the dead. 0, it was an awful day!

After this, all the Covenanter survivors of the battle were hunted out and killed, with especial ferocity; and when Claverhouse and his men were balked in their pursuit of one of them, they seized upon the first Presbyterian they could find, and put him to death, — so strangely bloodthirsty were they.

A very touching story I find in the history of this time, of the murder of one John Brown, a carrier, a brave and good man, — and of the Christian heroism of his wife, Marion. These two were married at a field-meeting, by a Mr. Peden, a celebrated preacher, who seems to have had the gift of prophecy ; for, after the ceremony, he said to Marion, solemnly: " You have got a good husband, — value him highly. Keep linen for a winding-sheet beside you; for in a day when you least expect it he may be taken from you!"

Three years after, this minister visited the carrier at his home, on the Farm of Priesthill, Ayrshire, and spent the night. The next day, when he was taking leave of Marion, he looked very sad, and said: " Poor woman, — a fearfud morning ! A dark and misty morning! "

When he was gone, John Brown took his spade and went out to his work, near the house. There was a thick mist, and the first the poor man knew he was sur-rounded by dragoons, with Cla-verhouse at their head. They began to question him sternly, and he answered readily and distinctly, which was strange, as always be-fore he had been troubled with a painful stammer. Cla-verhouse then called out to him: " Go to your prayers now, for the last time, — for you must die at once." John Brown knelt down, and prayed very fervently for himself and all men. Claverhouse interrupted him, impatiently, several times, and, when he closed, said: " Now say good night to your wife and children." John Brown turned to his wife, who stood near, with a baby in her arms and a little girl at her side, and said: " Now, Marion, the day is come that I told you might come, when I first spake to you of marrying me." She looked tenderly in his eyes, . and answered: " Indeed, John, in this cause I am willing to part with you." Then he kissed her and the babies, and blessed them.

Claverhouse commanded six soldiers to shoot him. Most of the bullets struck his head, and killed him instantly.

Marion had never before been able to see blood without fainting; but she did not faint at this fearful sight. Her eyes were only a little dazzled by the flash of the muskets. When all was over, Claverhouse said to her: " What thinkest thou of thy husband now, woman ? " She replied : " I always thought meikle (much) of him, and now more than ever."

When the cruel persecutors were gone, she set her baby down on the ground, tied up her husband's head with her kerchief, straightened his body, covered him over with her plaid, and then sat down and wept beside him.

The death of Charles the Second did not help the cause of the Covenanters much. They suffered persecution during the brief reign of his * bigoted brother, James the Second of England.

This king was a Catholic, and bent upon bringing both England and Scotland again under the yoke of the Pope. In the struggle with his rebellious subjects he lost his crown, and was forced to fly from his kingdom, while his daughter Mary and her husband (William, Prince of Orange), both Protestants, were called to the throne. These sovereigns wisely resolved to give full religious liberty to Scotland. In July, 1689, Prelacy was abolished in that country, and Pres-byterianism restored. So, after a long, stormy night of trouble and oppression, the sun of peace and tolera- tion arose upon poor Scotland.

The persecutions had lasted nearly a century, during which time no less than eighteen thousand people had suffered death, banishment, or long imprisonment; but the tears of anguish that were shed, and the hearts that were broken, only God can number. Let us thank him that such things can never be again, in a country calling itself Christian.

# THE TWO MARGARETS.

In May, 1685, during the reign of James the Seventh, two women, one named Margaret Mac-laughlin, and the other Margaret Wilson, were arrested for attending a field-meeting, and, refusing to conform, were sentenced to death. The first was an aged woman, weary of a world in which she had seen a great deal of trouble, and longing to depart and be with Christ. But the other, Margaret Wilson, was young, — only eighteen, and very fair. She had many to love her, for she loved many, and to her this earth seemed very beautiful. Yet she loved God better than life, — and went bravely, even cheerfully, to death for his sake.

The form of execution fixed upon for these two was singular, as well as very cruel. They were sentenced to be bound to stakes, driven down into the sea-beach, when the tide was coming in,— there to stand until the waters should overwhelm and drown them.

The morning when the people and the troops assembled on the sea-shore to see this sentence carried into execution was very bright and balmy. The blackbirds and thrushes, in the dark fir-trees, sang as gayly as ever, out of their glad, innocent hearts; tod the wild sea-birds, whirling in the pleasant air, screamed out their shrill delight, — while God's beautiful sunlight fell, as his rain and dew descend, " on the just, and on the unjust."

The two Margarets came down to the beach, escorted by a troop of rude sol-diers, and followed by a crowd of weeping friends. They both walked firmly and were very calm, though their faces were deadly pale, and their lips moved in prayer. Before they were fastened to the stakes, they were told that their lives would be spared, if they would, even then, renounce the Covenant. But again they firmly refused. Then they took a last leave of their friends.

Margaret Maclaughlin had children and grandchildren present. She kissed them and blessed them all, very tenderly and solemnly. One little grandson she took in her aged arms, and pressed to her bosom. He twined his chubby arms around her neck and cried, though he did not know why, only that he saw tears on her dear old cheeks. When she was led away to the stake, he struggled in his father's arms, and cried out: "Come back, grandmither! Dinna gang awa' into the black sea, — come back to Johnny!" This drew tears from many eyes in the crowd, and even touched the hard hearts of such of the soldiers as had children or grandchildren of their own.'

Margaret Wilson had to part with a father and mother, brothers and sisters. She was the calmest of them all, though she wept very much, especially when she parted from her mother, who was a sickly woman, and needed her help. This poor mother fainted in her husband's arms when their beloved daughter was led away by the soldiers. One of Margaret's brothers, a little boy, clung longest to her, sobbing and shrieking with passionate grief.

" Hush! hush! Jamie," said the young martyr ; " it breaks my heart to hear you; and if you fill my ears wi'yer loud greeting (weeping), I canna hear the whispers o' the angels wha come to strengthen me! "

Then Jamie grew still, let go her dress, and turned his face away. But when he saw her bound to the stake, and the waves rising around her, his wild grief broke out afresh, and he rushed into the water, crying: " I am a Covenanter, too, — I will go drown wi'my dear sister Maggie." He had to be brought back by force, and the incident so affected the spectators that many shouted, " Rescue the women ! Save them! save them! "

The military force was too strong for a rescue; but the people had hopes that they might bo saved, for the magistrate seemed to relent for a moment, and said that if the women would say, " God save the King!" they might go free. Then the people shouted to them to yield this much. " Consider," they said, " it is your duty to pray even for the greatest sinner! " " Ay, but not at the bidding of every profligate," replied brave old Margaret Maclaughlin. But as sweet Margaret Wilson said that she " wished not that any should perish, but that all should have everlasting life," they cried out that she had prayed for the king, and rushing into the water, brought her out. Then the magistrate, growing hard again, asked her sternly if she was ready now to renounce the Covenant. "No," she answered, with gentle firmness, "I have signed the Covenant, and I will abide by it for aye, wi' the help o' the God o' the Covenant." Then the magistrate grew very angry, and commanded that " the obstinate lass " should be taken back to the stake.

Then the two Margarets spoke cheering words to one another, and for a while looked towards the shore, smiling and waving their hands in loving farewell; but as the tide came in strong and stronger, they clasped their hands on their breasts, raised their eyes, and gave themselves up wholly to prayer.

The foaming waves rose to Margaret Wilson's slender waist, — over her gentle, noble heart,— above her white, praying hands; and they rose above Margaret Maclaughlin's strong, faithful-heart, — over her shrivelled, praying hands, trembling with cold; then, only two faces were seen, — one young and fair, the other old and wrinkled, — but both beaming with saintly glory ; and last, two heads of long hair — one gray, and the other golden — floated for a moment on the crest of a wave, and then sunk out of sight. The golden hair remained visible a little longer than the other; for, to the last, Margaret Wilson kept her . face turned towards Heaven, as though to wel-come the angels coming to receive her soul; but old Margaret Maclaughlin closed her eyes, and let her bead sink on her breast, as though she wished to be carried sleeping to her Father's mansion, in the arms of angels, like a wearied child. When all was over, it happened that a little wave brought to Jamie Wilson's feet the snood, or white ribbon, which had confined his sister's beautiful hair. He caught it up, kissed it, wept over it, hid it next his heart, and ever after treasured it as the relic of a saint.

Edinburgh.

# THE 'PRENTICE'S PILLAR.

BEFORE quitting altogether tho subject of tho unhappy religious strife which so long desolated Scotland, I will relate two charming stories, from history, which may show you how nobly heroic gentle-hearted . women, even young girls, may be, in times of war and persecution.

It happens that both of my heroines were called Grizel,— not a very pretty name, certainly, but I think you will grow to liking it, after reading of them. I will begin with

# GRIZEL HUME.

A short time before the death of Charles the Second, there was an enterprise formed by several eminent English and Scottish lords and gen-tlemen, to prevent the Duke of York, afterwards James the Second, of England, from ascending the throne. Through treachery and rashness this enterprise failed, and many of those engaged in it were arrested and put to death. Among the few leaders who escaped the vengeance of the government was the good and brave Sir Patrick Hume, of Polwarth. It happened that the party of soldiers sent to arrest him stopped for re-freshment at the house of a nobleman known to be loyal. Here they inquired the way to Polwarth Castle, and their hostess, being a friend to Sir Patrick, resolved to give him warning. She did not dare to write, nor even to trust one of her servants to carry a plain message to her neighbor; but, being very ingenious, she took an eagle's feather, and wrapping it in a piece of blank paper, sent it by a fleet-footed Highland boy across the hills to Polwarth. She then put wines and rich meats before her guests, and made them all feel so extremely comfortable that they lingered at her house as long as possible.

Sir Patrick understood at once, from the token she sent, that he was in danger, and must fly or secrete himself. He resolved upon the latter course as the least hazardous, and could think of no safer hiding-place than a vault in Polwarth church-yard, where his ancestors were buried. It was a dismal place enough, — damp, dark, and cold, — with dead men and women and children lying all about in mouldering coffins, covered with tattered black palls; but it was better than a prison cell, chains, and a scaffold. Soarcely had he secreted himself before the soldiers arrived. They searched for him high and low, far and wide, ---everywhere but in the old vault. Then they separated and went off in various directions, still searching, inquiring, and swearing at their ill luck. At night, a faithful domestic carried a bed and some blankets to the church-yard, flung them down into the vault, and then ran home, his heart beating loud, and his teeth chattering for fear of ghosts and hobgoblins.

But there was one who was not frightened from her duty by any such wild fancies, so full was her heart of that "perfect love which casteth out fear." This was Sir Patrick's daughter, Grizel, a beautiful young lady, only eighteen, but thought-ful, courageous, and prudent beyond her years. She was the only one who could be trusted to carry her' father his food, which must always be taken to him at mid-night. Her mother, who was rather afflicted With cowardice, —" nervousness " she called it, — waited for her return in dreadful anxiety, and when she came, took her in her arms, blessed her and rejoiced over her as though she had risen from the dead. "But did it no fright you, lassie, to pass through the kirk-yard at such an aw-ful time o' night ?" she asked. " No, no, mother," said Grizel, smiling; " I knew God could take care of me as well at midnight as at noonday, and I felt that every star above was a kind angel's face, watching over me. I feared nothing, mother, but the minister's dogs, lest their barking should rouse the people at the manse, and dear father's hiding-place be discovered."

The next day Lady Hume sent for the minister, and complaining of a fear of mad dogs (I am afraid she stretched a point there), persuaded him to shut up his dogs for a time.

Grizel had a good deal of trouble in obtaining food for her father without the knowledge of the servants, whom it was thought not best to trust with her secret. She used to watch her chance and take pieces of meat and bread from the table, when the family were at dinner. One day, when they had sheep's head, a good old Scotch dish, Grizel took a larger portion than usual off the platter, and hid it in her napkin. Scarcely had she done so when one of her brothers, a little boy, and, like other little boys, apt to blunder out the wrong thing at the wrong time and place, bawled out indignantly, " O mamma, see Grizzy! while we were supping the broth, she has eaten up almost all the sheep's head." The poor girl feared that her secret would be discovered then, but the servants present only wondered what had come over Miss Grizel, to be so greedy.

Sir Patrick remained in the funeral vault, with no light by day but what came through a little hole at one end, and no amusement but reading and reciting psalms, for several weeks; then he ventured to return for a little while to his house, and from there he made his escape in safety to Holland, where he remained till after the death of Charles the Second.

# GRIZEL COCHRANE.

Sir John Cochrane, of Ochiltree, a son of the Earl of Dundonald, and a most heroic gentleman, was engaged with Sir Patrick Hume in the conspiracy against the Duke of York. He also made his escape to Holland, and, with his friend and other patriotic refugees, returned to join a rebellion, headed by the Duke of Argyle, against James the Second. This, like the other plot, was unsuccessful. The Duke, as you have seen, suffered death; and Sir John Cochrane was arrested, tried, and condemned to die, though great efforts were made to save him by his father, the Earl of Dundonald, who had never conspired against the government.

No friend or relative was allowed to see the prisoner until after his condemnation, when he was informed by his surly jailer, that, during the time which must pass before the arrival of the death-warrant from London, he might see his family. Sir John, however, not being willing to bring upon his sons the suspicion of sharing his treason, sent them his positive commands to refrain from visiting him until the night before his execution; but he said his beloved only daughter, Grizel, a fair girl of eighteen, might visit him at once, if she would ; and she came. Her beautiful, loving face seemed almost to bring the dear-ness and peace of home, the brightness and sweetness of liberty into his dreary cell, though it was pale and worn with sorrow, and overflowed with tears. Grizel flung herself upon her father's breast and sobbed bitterly; but when she felt the tears of that strong, brave man falling on her hand, she hushed her sobs, and strove to comfort him.

She told him her grandfather, the Earl, had petitioned the king for a pardon, and would make a strong effort to obtain the favor of his Majesty's confessor, the powerful Father Peters. But Sir John shook his head despondingly, saying that even if the king could be persuaded to forgive such a notorious rebel, the pardon would not probably arrive at Edinburgh till several days after the death-warrant had come and all was over.

Every day Grizel visited her father, and talked with him about these matters, and every night she spent many waking hours in striving to contrive some plan for his deliverance. The only thing to be done, it seemed to her, was to intercept or delay the death-warrant, so that the friends who were working for him in London could have time to effect their good purpose. But *how* to do this was the question. At last, a few days before the warrant was expected by the council in Edinburgh, she fixed upon a bold plan for getting possession of it. She did not confide this plan to any, not even to her father. She only told him very quietly that some important business would prevent her from visiting him for a day or two. Yet he was some-what alarmed, and replied: " Don't, my dear daughter, undertake any plan to save me, for which your age and sex unfit you."

" I am a Cochrane, my father," she replied; " do not fear for me." Still, for all her heroism, her heart sunk, and her tears fell fast, when the prison-door closed on that poor father. What if she had taken her last look of his beloved face!

The next morning early Grizel assumed a humble disguise, mounted a favorite palfrey, and rode out of Edinburgh towards the borders. She stopped only at country cottages, where she passed herself off as a housemaid taking a journey to visit her friends. On the second day, she reached the house of her old nurse, who lived just over the Tweed, near the town of Berwick. To this woman she revealed her secret, and the good dame promised to aid her all in her power, though she shook her head sadly, and said it was an awful undertaking. And so it was ; for Grizel's purpose was no other than to waylay and rob the postman of the mail! hoping thus to get possession of the warrant. She had brought with her a brace of pistols and a horseman's cloak; and her nurse lent her a suit of clothes belonging to her son, Grizel's foster-brother, which luckily fitted the brave girl very well.

In those times, the mail was brought from London to Edinburgh on horseback, — the bags containing it being strapped on to the saddle before the postman, who was always armed. The journey took full eight days; so Grizel cal-culated that if she could carry out her plan, it would be at least sixteen or seventeen days before a second death-warrant could be received, which, she hoped, would afford her father's friends a fair opportunity to obtain his pardon. She had somehow ascertained that the postman was in the habit of stopping at a little inn kept by a widow, near Bedford, on a certain day, to take a few hours' rest. He usually reached this place in the early morning, and Grizel contrived to arrive a short time after he had breakfasted and laid down to sleep. She put up her horse, and, going into the house, asked for some refreshment.

" Well, sit down at that table, my bonnie lad," replied the landlady, " and I will serve you; but please be as quiet as possible, for there is the London postman asleep in that bed, and I would not have him disturbed."

After making a slight meal, Grizel asked for some fresh water, offering to pay for it the price of good beer; and, while the dame was gone to the well, she rose, and stole on tip-toe to the bed on which the postman was sleeping. To her disappointment, he was lying with the mail-bags under his head and shoulders; and she saw that she could not take them away without waking him. By his side, lay his pistols. She had just time to draw the loading from these, and put them back into the holsters, before the landlady returned. Then she paid liberally for her breakfast, and, having carelessly asked how long the postman would be likely to sleep, she mounted her horse and rode away in a direction opposite to the one she came from.

She took a cir cuit, however, and came out on the high road, when she ambled along slowly until the postman came up. Then she checked her horse, and fell into a conversation with him. He was a large, burly man, but with a good-natured face, and, Grizel was glad to see, not a very brave or determined-looking fellow.

Miss Cochrane watched her opportunity, and when they came to a lonely place, near a wood, with no house or traveller in sight, she rode close to her companion, and said, sternly: "Friend, I have taken a fancy to those mail-bags, and I must have them, at all hazards. I am armed, well mounted, and determined to have my will. So, take my advice, give up the mail-bags, and go back the way you came ; and, if you value your life, don't come near yonder wood for at least two hours."

The stout postman only burst into a hearty fit of laughter at this. " 0 ho, my pretty youth!" he said, " you are disposed to make yourself merry at my expense! Deliver up his Majesty's mails to one like you, forsooth! Go, to! you look more fit to rob birds' nests and orchards. If I were churlish enough to take offence at a boy's foolish jest, I could teach you a hard lesson, Master Smooth-face." As he said this, he saw something in Grizel's eye which did not look like jesting, — so, taking a pistol from the holster and cocking it, he added: " But if you are mad enough to be in earnest, I am ready for you, you see, — so put spurs to your horse and be off with you, while you have a whole skin."

It was a perilous moment for Grizel. She knew it was possible that the man had discovered her trick at the inn, and had reloaded his pistols; but she thought of her father, and did not flinch. " I don't like to shed blood," she said, " but I am also ready;" and, drawing a pistol and presenting it, " *that mail I must and will have* ! So, take your choice, — deliver it, or die !"

" Well, then, you hair-brained stripling, your blood be on your own head!" cried the postman, firing his pistol, which only flashed in the pan. He flung it down, seized the other, fired, — and again there was only a flash! Then, in a rage, he leaped to the ground, and tried to seize her horse by the reins,—but, by the quick use of the spur, she escaped from his grasp, and, before he was aware of her purpose, she caught his own horse, and was galloping off with it, mail-bags and all! She looked back once, to point her pistol at him. and warn him not to follow her, — then she put both horses to their utmost speed, till she reached the wood, — when she left the highway, and rode into the deepest part of the forest. Here she tied the post-man's horse to a tree, unstrapped the mail-bags, cut them open with her penknife, and took out the Government despatches, which she knew by their great seals. Among these she found not only her father's death-warrant, but several others, all of which she tore into small pieces -and hid in her bosom. She then replaced the other papers in the mail-bags (where they were afterwards found), mounted her horse, returned to the house of her nurse, burned the fragments of the warrants, resumed her female dress, and journeyed back to Edinburgh, all in perfect safety.

Her heroic act did indeed save the life of her father. It gave the Earl of Dundon-ald time to persuade Father Peters (with the help of five thousand pounds) to per-suade the king that it would be for the good of his royal soul to pardon his enemy, Sir John Cochrane, — and he did it.

This is the only instance I remember to have ever heard of, where robbing the mail was justifiable. Yet I hardly think it a piece of heroism which would bear repeating.

I hope that Miss Hume and Miss Cochrane, the two Grizels, were good friends. They ought to have been.

# THE ENVIRONS OP EDINBURGH.

There are many places in the vicinity of Edinburgh which travellers should visit, not only for their beauty, but because their names are familiar to all readers of Scottish history, poetry, romance. A few miles from the city, on the river Esk, in the green depths of a lovely dell, stands the Gothic Chapel, of Roslin, built several centuries ago, by the St. Clairs, Earls of Caithness and Orkney, and Lords of Roslin, — who dwelt near by, in a stately castle.

The castle is now but a grand old ruin, — the proud and warlike lords who once inhabited it lie beneath the Chapel, each clad in a complete suit; of armor, an iron shroud, — the strong arm, the bloody hand, the fiery heart, the haughty voice, still and silent forever; but the Chapel, the best of all their works, lives after them,— remains yet beautiful, august, and solemn,— seeming almost to consecrate their stern memories,— to atone for many sins, to rise over their poor dust like a perpetual intercession for their souls.

The architecture of the chapel is of different styles, representing the tastes and art of the different ages in which it was built. The ornamental portions are of wonderful variety and beauty, — displaying a thousand forms of curious and graceful sculpture. Among the columns which support the stately arches, is one so beautiful in form and so perfect in finish, that all tourists pause before it in surprise, and linger long to admire it, — marvelling at the genius which created such a joy for the eye out of the dull, rude rock, — which carved such a poem in stone. This pillar is completely wreathed with foliage, so delicately modelled, so exquisitely wrought, that, hard and colorless as it is, you almost fancy it can stir and rustle, and send out faint fragrance on the air.

But there is something beside its beauty to make one remember this pillar. It is a legend, dark and sorrowful, which clings about it as closely as its lovely sculptures, and will cling as long,

## THE LEGEND OP THE 'PRENTICE'S PILLAR.

The master-builder of Roslin Chapel was a hard, ambitious man, who thought only of the fame and fortune his work would win for him, — not of the glory of the Holy One to whom the edifice would be dedicated, or of the sacred joy which devout souls would have in worshipping within it. He did not even love the grand arches and pillars, the figures of saints and angels, and the sweet little cherub faces he planned and sculptured, — save as he counted up how much gold and renown they would bring him, — so that it seemed that, while turning stones into beauty and worship, he had turned his heart into stone. When erecting the high altar itself, he wrought more for the honor of his own name than for that of his heavenly Lord, — and if he had dared, he would have set up his own scowling effigy in some lofty niche, in place of the statue of a meek-browed saint or angel, for the people to bend before in solemn reverence.

This man was not only thus arrogant and selfish, but bitterly jealous of the talent and fame of other architects, treating them all as though they were his natural enemies, whose very presence, even while he made use of their labor, was a wrong and an offence.

There was among his apprentices one whom he especially hated, because he could not help seeing that the youth had great genius for his art, and was likely to be very famous. This young sculptor was of a nature gentle, generous, and devout, and bore himself quietly and meekly under his hard master's taunts and reproofs. He consoled himself for all such little trials, by the delight he took in his art. He loved to reproduce, in imperishable marble, the fading forms of earthly beauty, — flowers, and foliage, and lovely childish faces, and he loved best of all to labor for the adornment of noble edifices, dedicated to Him who inspired worship and created all beautiful things. He thought he saw in nature the types of great cathedrals, — in the solemn arches of dim forests, in the mighty boles of ancient oaks, in the rocky towers of mountain-steeps, in gorgeous sunset clouds — the stained windows of heaven.

It happened that the master-builder found him-self unable to make a certain pillar, after a plan which had been brought from Rome, without going all the way to that city, to examine the model. The journey was a tedious and perilous one in those days, yet the ambitious artisan undertook it, — saying nothing of his purpose to any one.

During his absence, the young apprentice came across the plans which his master had not understood, but which were clear to his keen, beauty-loving eyes, and, thinking no harm, began to work them out. Every morning, before he commenced his work, he prayed that good angels might guide his chisel; every evening he walked alone in the fields and woods, and reverently studied the foliage of trees and vines, that he might be able to copy them exactly, to the curl of a tendril, or the most delicate veining of a leaf. Every flower bore for his eyes traces of the hand of the Divine Artist, — every smallest spray conveyed a lesson from the great Master-Builder of the universe.

All alone he toiled, till a magic summer began to bud and blossom out of the cold, hard stone,— fair, white forms of flower and foliage, which one might fancy lovely ghosts of old-world bloom and verdure, that perished by flood or fire, and were embedded or fused in the fluid rock, — came forth, day by day, and seemed to climb and wreathe themselves around the graceful pillar.

At last it was finished and raised to its place, to the sound of a hymn, sung by the pious young artisan; and while everybody was wondering and admiring, the master-builder came home, full of his project for delighting the Lord of Roslin and all Scotland, by the marvellous pillar he was about to execute.

It happened that the first of his workmen whom he met was the young apprentice.

"Well, sirrah," said he, scornfully, "what have you been about while I have been away? Anything better than idle dreaming? "

" Yes, my master," replied the youth, modestly, "I have executed a pillar, from some plans I found in your study; and I hope my work will please you."

" *A pillar*! Show it to me. I warrant it must come down right speedily. A pillar, forsooth! and after my plans. How dare you meddle with matters above your condition? "

The apprentice did not reply, but quietly led his master to the pillar, and stood by, longing, yet hardly daring to hope for his approval. For some moments, the master-builder stood still, overwhelmed with amazement. Here was that difficult design which he had travelled so far, and braved so many dangers to study, wrought out more admirably than he could have executed it,— a finer work even than the model at Rome, — and all this done by a mere apprentice, whom he had rated and flouted a thousand times! Then he was seized with a mad fit of jealous rage at having lost the fame he had taken such pains to secure, and, catching up a heavy mallet that lay near, he struck the apprentice to the ground.

It was the poor youth's death-blow." He lay quite still, the blood gushing from a ghastly wound in his broad, white forehead, and darkly staining the rich golden curls of his hair. , But he revived for a moment, feebly turned his head, fixed his eyes mournfully, yet fondly, upon his last beautiful work, and murmured: " I meant it for God's glory, master, and your gain ;" and so died.

Those were days of lawless violence; and the legend does not go on to tell that a coroner's inquest was held over the body of the poor apprentice, or that the master-builder was arrested, tried, and executed for his untimely taking off. Perhaps the man had Mends, rich and respectable, who hushed up the unpleasant little matter; perhaps he was wanted to build more churches. Doubtless he would have liked to remove that pillar, but dared not, as it was now not only a beautiful part of the sacred edifice, but a monument to the innocent dead.

But the place where it stood must ever have been for him a sad and haunted spot. It is not likely that he fancied much passing near it after dark. If his duties ever compelled him to visit the chapel at night, though he entered with ever so bold a brow and defiant a spirit, there entered with him Remorse, like an avenging angel, and everything he beheld seemed to speak of his crime. The beautiful stained windows changed the mild moonlight into ghastly gleams. The shadows under the great arches seemed full of threatening and horror. The little cherub-faces above the pillars seemed to put on looks of affright at beholding him, and Madonna to draw the holy child nearer to her protecting bosom. "The pale saints in their niches, by the stillness of their eternal calm, seemed to reprove him for his unholy pas-sions, and the piteous figure of the Lord himself, by its mute agony on the cross, to reproach him for his cruelty. Surely, the marble of that memorial pillar, gleaming in the dim light, recalled to him the death whiteness of a face, which neither coffin-lid, nor earth, nor stone could long shut away from the eyes of his soul. Though fearing and hating that stern, inexorable witness of his sin, he would perhaps linger long to gaze upon it, awe-struck by its silent, accusing beauty, till the snowy flowers immortally blossoming around it, would redden in his sight, and seem to drip with a dreadful dew, the blood his hand had shed in that holy place.

Near Roslin, is Hawthornden, one of the loveliest places in all Scotland, once the seat of Drum-mond, a poet of the time of Elizabeth. A little way down the river is the village of Lasswade, — so called after a stout *lass*, who once on a time used to carry travellers across the ford on her back. I think she must have been related to good St. Christopher, or to Strongback, the friend of Prince Fortunatus.

Other beautiful and interesting places in the vicinity of Edinburgh are Melville Castle, Dalkeith Palace, Newbattle Abbey, Dalhousie House, and Borthwick Castle ; a fine old fortress, famous as the place where Queen Mary and the Earl of Bothwell spent a part of their honeymoon, if so sweet a name can be given to the unhappy time they lived together. Mary escaped from this castle in the disguise of a page, and fled to Dunbar. Then there is Crichton Castle, on the Tyne, — which is described in Walter Scott's poem of "*Marmion*" — Oxenford Castle, and the ruins of Cragmillar Castle, once a favorite residence of Queen Mary.

Charming excursions can be made in every direction from Edinburgh; you cannot go amiss. First in interest are Abbotsford, Dryburgh, and Melrose; but I will speak of these in another chapter. At Jedburgh there is an old Abbey, thought to be the most magnificent ruin in Scotland ; at Kelso, there is another ruined abbey. Then there is battered old Norham Castle, and if you have enough of ruins, there are the lovely vales of Yarrow and Ettrick and Teviotdale, that we read so much about in Scottish poetry and romance.

There is a fine old town, about twenty miles from Edinburgh, called Peebles, which I was sorry not to see. It is scarcely mentioned in history. except as a place sometimes visited by the king and court, because of its pleasant situation in a good hunting country, on the road to the royal forest of Ettrick. It is the scene of a poem by James the First, and of a touching little tradition told by Walter Scott and other poets, far better than I can tell it; however I will do my best.

# THE LAIRD'S RETURN.

Many years ago, when Nidpath Castle, near Peebles, was inhabited by the Earl of March, — a son of the Duke of Queensbury, — a young lady of that proud family became very tenderly attached to the Laird of Tushielaw in Ettrick Forest ; but when the lover waited on the Earl and Countess, to ask the hand of Lady Mary in marriage, it was refused with anger and scorn. A daughter of their noble house, they said, must never descend to wed a simple Scotch Laird. The Countess, in whose veins there ran real royal blood, though considerably diluted, was particularly incensed at such presumption. She grew red and then white; she frowned and swelled and tossed her head in high-bred contempt. Even her rich silk robe seemed to rustle indignantly, and her lace ruff to bristle up at the young Laird, while a bright red jewel which she wore on her forehead, set in a band of gold, seemed to glare at him angrily, like a little fiery eye. But Scott of Tushielaw stood his ground manfully. He said that, though not a noble, he was a gentleman, and the son of a gentleman, and held that an alliance with him would not disgrace the proudest family in the kingdom. Then he left them, declaring that he would only take his dismissal from Lady Mary herself. The angry parents next summoned their daughter, and sternly accused her of a great crime, in loving out of the nobility. She pleaded guilty, and prayed for their consent to marry young Scott, shocking them very much by saying that she would rather be happy with his love, than wretched with a title and a coronet. Of course they refused, and set themselves, by commands, reproaches, and harsh treatment, to cause her to reject her lover. At last they got their Father Confessor to deal with her. Very solemnly he argued, and warned her against the sin of disobedience ; for Heaven, he said, was always on the side of the parents in such cases, — especially parents of the nobility. Yet nothing he said seemed to move her, till he declared that if she persisted in marrying Tushielaw, she would bring the curse of the Church upon him, and so put his soul in peril. Then Lady Mary, being young and superstitious, burst into tears, and sobbed out, " O Father Ambrose, don't say any more! I *will* give him up! "

So she wrote a sorrowful little letter of farewell to Scott of Tushielaw, while the priest stood over her and blessed her. The Countess of March sent her page in such haste with that letter, that the tears poor Lady Mary dropped on it were hardly dry when it reached the young Laird's hands. It seemed to pierce his heart like a sharp dagger; yet he kissed it tenderly, and his own eyes grew dim over the words which had so wounded him. He treasured it up and took it with him abroad, where he went to find what comfort he could in foreign travel.

From the day of his going, Lady Mary drooped and faded, pining for the kind smile and the gentle words of the one she loved best of all the world. She lost her own gay smile, — her tones grew sad, her step slow, and the sweet red color went out from her cheeks and lips. Then there came a cough,—a very little cough, which scarcely shook the muslin kerchief on her neck, but which sounded of death as surely as a funeral knell. Nothing revived or comforted her,—not the coming of the spring, with leaves and flowers, — not balls, nor hunting, — not even the homage of a great noble, a real Duke, who offered her his coronet, his castle, and his heart.

At last she took to her couch, and the little cough went on, and wasted her day by day, till even the Earl and Countess saw that Death, and not the Duke, was coming for their daughter. They confessed to each other that there was but one hope for her, — the recall of her lover. It was a hard remedy for them, — next to death, but they submitted; for, after all, they loved their gentle child, in their way, — and they wrote to the young Laird to come home, saying that they would now give him the hand of the Lady Mary.

Scott was as proud as they; but his pride was of a nobler kind, and he did not refuse to come. He wrote to Lady Mary a glad, loving letter, and named the very day on which she might look for him at Nidpath Castle. When this letter came, the poor girl strove to rise from her couch and take into her heart the joy of life and love once more. But she was like a delicate lily, which, after its stem was broken, should try to lift its head towards the sun, and to catch the dew in its withered cup.

It was too late!

On the afternoon of the day when her lover was to arrive, Lady Mary caused herself to be carried to a house belonging to her family, in the town of Peebles, through which the young Laird would pass on his way to the Castle. She could meet him so much the sooner, she said.

A softly cushioned chair was placed for her on a stone balcony, over the gateway of the mansion, and here she sat, with her mother and her maids, looking and listening, till the summer sun was setting, and the twilight shadows began to creep over the hills. She seemed to listen with her heart, for long before the others could distinguish a sound, she heard the gallop of a steed, coming nearer and nearer; and then, for in the distance, saw and knew the rider, and clasping her hands, she cried: " It is he! It is he! 0 mother, God is so good to me!"

It seemed hours, though it was not many minutes, before the Laird reached the Queensbury house, and came riding along just beneath the balcony. Lady Mary now stood without support, and her glad heart sent a little glow of welcome to her wan cheeks. The traveller raised his head and looked full in her face, and she bent forward and smiled on him tenderly, like a sweet pale star out of heaven. But alas! he had no thought of her being so changed by sorrow and illness. The face seemed like the shadow of one he had seen, or it was one he had dreamed of; he could not think it hers. His heart was so full of memories of the round, healthful form, and the bright, rosy face of his Mary, as he had loved her first, that he did not know her now. So he only gave her a brief, cold, strange look, and galloped on. Lady Mary uttered a wild, mournful cry ; " O mother," she said, " he has forgotten me! forgotten me!" and sunk back into her chair, softly, but white and cold as marble.

" Help! " cried the Countess of March, " she has fainted."

That wild, sad cry had reached the ear of her lover, and he knew her voice. Instantly he sprang from his horse and hurried to the balcony, where she still sat, with her weeping friends around her. He took her in his arms and kissed her, and

called her " Mary," Still she did not stir or speak. " Help!" cried the Countess again, "bring a doctor!" But there was no
help for her — she was dead!

When the young Laird saw that it was indeed so, he knelt by her side, and laid his face in her lap, and took one of her thin, white hands in his, and sorrowed over it.

So it *was* Death, and not the great Duke, — Death, and not the humble Laird,— who came for the lovely daughter of the Earl and Countess of March. Not with the whiteness and brightness of bridal robes and flowers, — not with the fast ringing of merry marriage-bells, pealing out louder and louder, and breaking in upon one another like a group of happy young villagers, in haste to tell each other some joyful news,— but with the black pomp of funeral ceremonies, and with the slow ringing of the solitary chapel bell, lengthening out each heavy toll, as though sorry and afraid to repeat its mournful story.

It was for Lady Mary's sake I wished to visit Peebles and Nidpath Castle.

The City Cross.

THE "PRETENDERS."

NEAR the Royal Exchange Buildings, Edinburgh, formerly stood a large stone cross, which surmounted an eight-sided turret. It was demolished in 1756, and its destruction has always been thought a foolish act of bigotry. Sir Walter Scott was especially indignant about it. From this cross, for several centuries, royal edicts, new laws, and sovereigns were proclaimed, with blowing of trumpets. The last Scottish king ' here proclaimed was the Chevalier de St. George, — or " the Pretender," as he was called by the English, — under the title of James the Eighth of Scotland, and third of England, by order of his son, Charles Edward, acting as Prince Regent. In this chapter I will endeavor to give you a condensed history of these two remarkable royal personages, and so have done with the Stuarts.

JAMES.

You will recollect that after King James the Second was driven from his home and kingdom, he was succeeded by his daughter, Mary, and her husband, William of Orange, a Protestant Prince. On the death of King William, who survived his wife several years, Queen Mary's sister, the Princess Anne, ascended the throne. Her father had died in exile, after bequeathing his rights to his eldest son, who bore the foreign title of the Chevalier de St. George. Queen Anne had no children at the time of her accession to the throne, and her Protestant counsellors, who were anxious to bar out the Catholic Stuarts, advised her to have the succession fixed upon a distant relative, George, the Elector of Hanover, who was a Protestant. Queen Anne long hesitated. Her heart secretly yearned towards her brother, and she sometimes felt cruel remorse for the course she had taken towards her father, in turning against him, and accepting the crown which had been forcibly taken from his poor, obstinate old head. But she hardly had courage to propose to her Protestant subjects a Catholic king, and as the Chevalier was as fanatically devoted to his religion as his father had been, there was little hope of his coming round to the right point.

When James the Second escaped to Prance, he was very courteously received by the great king, Louis the Fourteenth, who assigned him a palace at St. Germain, near Paris. Here he lived, in a sort of idle mimicry of royal state, plotting and intriguing, and always expecting that something would " turn up " to restore him the crown and kingdom which he had lost by his stupid tyranny. His court was composed of exiled nobles and their wives, — poor and proud, — mercenary soldiers, reckless adventurers, and plenty of priests, I assure you. Here the young Prince James was brought up. He was constantly taught that he was the rightful heir to the British crown, and that he must regain it from the usurpers ; yet he was not well instructed in the duties of a king, or a revolutionary leader. He was a tall, handsome man, courteous and elegant in his manners, and naturally kind and amiable; but he lacked boldness, energy, and a strong will. In short, he would have made a very nice, agreeable private gentleman, but there was little of the real kingly stuff about him.

When old King James was on his death-bed, and very near his end, he sent word to Louis the Fourteenth that he desired to see him. The "***Grand Monarque***" as he was called, came in great state, as he used to go everywhere, — all in velvet, brocade, and gold, — high-heeled shoes, lace and diamonds, and in an enormous wig, that would have quite put out any other man, like an extinguisher. So he came to the dying king, and his flattering courtiers said that the sight of him was enough to awe Death himself, and drive him out of that chamber.

The old king partly raised himself in bed, to receive his magnificent visitor, whom he thanked for all his kindness; and when the French king graciously waved his hand, as much as to say, " There is no occasion for gratitude, I have really done next to nothing,"—James, calling the young Prince to his side, continued: " Yet for all your kindness, my dear royal brother, I must leave you but a troublesome legacy, — my son and his fortunes. Show to him, I pray you, the same magnanimous friendship you have shown to me, discrowned and despoiled of my kingly rights. Promise me this, and receive the blessing of a dying man."

" I promise," replied Louis. " I will take him and his under my protection. I will recognize his right to the throne of Britain, — I will aid him in winning his crown. So, my brother, depart in peace,—if you really must go."

On hearing this, James was affected to tears, though being a king, he ought to have known what king's promises were worth; his courtiers also wept,—the young Chevalier wept, and even the great Louis put his embroidered handkerchief . to his eyes, — when, as it was ***his*** courtiers' duty to believe that he was weeping copiously, they entirely broke down, and abandoned themselves to tears of admiration and grief.

When King Louis had composed himself, he bade King James a solemn adieu, and swept from the chamber in all his glory and majesty, — and then it did seem as if Death had been waiting respectfully in the anteroom, and only came in when he went out; for King James began to sink immediately. He bade an affectionate farewell to his family and court, then turned to his confessor, and taking his crucifix, pressed it to his lips, and said prayer after prayer till he died.

This generous and solemn promise of Louis the Fourteenth gave great encouragement to the Jacobites, as the adherents of the Stuarts were called, from Jacobus, the Latin for James. After much delay and many secret negotiations, Louis actually furnished the Chevalier with an army of five thousand men, and despatched him to Dunkirk, where he was to sail for Scotland, in a fleet under the command of the Count de Forbin. Could they have sailed at once, the enterprise might have been successful, as a large party in Scotland were favorable to it, and England was illy prepared to resist it, the greater part of her army being in Flanders. But, just then, the luckless Chevalier was taken down with the measles, — a bad enough disease under any circumstances, but in this case it may have lost the Prince a kingdom; for it gave the English time to prepare so well for the invasion, by land and sea, that, though the French fleet actually reached the Frith of Forth, the Count de Forbin refused to land the Chevalier and his troops, but took them all back to France as speedily as possible. Louis seems to have thought that he had redeemed his promise, or his memory was remarkably short, for not long afterwards he signed a treaty, called " the treaty of Utrecht," in which he acknowledged Queen Anne's right to the throne, and actually agreed to expel her brother from his dominions. So poor James was obliged to seek another refuge. For some time he cherished hopes that his sister Anne would help to restore his rights to him; but, as I have said, though her heart favored him, she lacked courage to avow her wish, and she died without naming him as her successor. The English people imported their next sovereign, — the Elector of Hanover, — who reigned under the title of George the First. After him came three other Georges, then William the Fourth, then Queen Victoria, the best and most beloved of the race. This change of royal families is what is meant by the " Hanoverian succession."

King George did not behave in a magnanimous or politic way towards the Scottish Jacobites. He even refused to receive a loyal address from several Highland chiefs, represented by the Earl of Mar. By so doing, he offended them all, and especially Mar, whom he afterwards found a very troublesome enemy.

In September, 1715, many Jacobite nobles and gentlemen assembled at Aboyne, and proclaimed the Chevalier de St. George King of England, Ireland, and their dependencies, under the title of James the Third, and of Scotland under that of James the Eighth. The leaders set about raising a revolutionary army at once. The Highland chiefs, as you know, were supreme rulers of their clans: they did not invite, but commanded them to rally and fight for their true prince.

After an ancient custom, they raised recruits by sending " the fiery cross" through the different clans. This cross was composed of two branches of wood, one partly burned with fire and the other stained with blood, — to signify that, if any Scot to whom it should be sent should fail to present himself at a certain place, which should be named to him, he would be punished by fire and sword. This symbol was sent from house to house, and man to man, and none dared to disregard it. Yet few of the Highlanders needed any threats at this time. Most of them were passionately attached to the cause of the Stuarts, were dissatisfied with the union with England, and disgusted with the new king.

The Jacobites took the town of Perth, which gave them great advantages,—but unfortunately, their leader, Mar, was a poor general, and most of the other chiefs were more brave and enthusiastic than skilful or prudent. There were useless delays, — there were mistakes and disagreements, and no decisive engagement took place till the battle of Sheriffmuir was fought in No-vember. Both armies claimed the victory, but the Jacobites lost by far the most men, and were obliged to retreat, which surely was as like being beaten as possible.

About the same time fourteen hundred of the rebel forces were surrounded at Preston, and compelled to surrender. The leaders were con-ducted to London, bound like felons, and many of them put to death. They suffered bravely, for as a general thing these adherents of the Stuarts were grandly heroic men.

At last, in December, 1715, the Chevalier himself arrived. He had embarked at Dunkirk, in the disguise of a sailor, with only six followers, also disguised, on a small vessel loaded with a cargo of brandy. Yet he failed to impart *spirits* to the Jacobites. Things had been so badly managed,— all felt so discouraged by defeat, and weakened, as it were, by the loss of so much noble blood, shed in vain, — that not even the presence of him they believed their rightful king could give them hope and strengh. Moreover, the Chevalier himself was disheartened and ill. It was not the measles this time but the ague, which seemed to have shaken all the courage and will out of him. After a few miserable attempts at royalty and generalship, but without fighting a single battle, he abandoned the enterprise, and, with the Earl of Mar, escaped to the Continent, leaving his army, beset by a powerful force under the Duke of Argyle, to save themselves if they could.

So ended the rebellion of 1715 ; a humiliating termination, which one would suppose might have cured the Scots of their mad attachment to the Stuarts, but it did not.

# CHARLES EDWARD.

Soon after the Chevalier returned to the Continent, he married the Princess Clementina Sobi-eski, of Poland, the heiress to an immense fortune, who thought, simple girl, that she was making a magnificent marriage, and doubtless looked forward to sharing the throne of Great Britain with her husband, now poor, powerless, crownless, and hunted from all the courts of Europe, the Pope's excepted.

There were two children from this marriage. Charles Edward, born in 1720, to whom the Jacobites gave the title of Prince of Wales, — and, five years after, Benedict, Duke of York, who entered the Church, and was made a cardinal.

Charles Edward was bred up to win back the lost crown of the Stuarts; and as soon as he grew to manhood, he was urged on to his great work. Poor fellow, he was worthy of a better fate, — for he was by nature noble, brave, persevering, kind-hearted, and affable. He was tall, fair, and handsome, though his face had rather a melancholy expression. But he was not much better calculated to make a good king than his father. He knew little of the science of government, or the true character of the English people. Be-sides being a zealous Papist, he was a devout believer in the " divine right of kings " to do precisely as they pleased in all things, and at all times,—a false and foolish doctrine, which cost his father and grandfather a crown, and his greatgrandfather his head beside. He was haughty and extremely selfish, though always courteous, and sometimes very gentle and winning in his manner.

The king and the prince — or the Chevalier de St. George and the Chevalier Douglas, or the two Pretenders — kept up a secret correspondence with the English and Scottish Jacobites for several years, and on the first opportunity which seemed at all favorable, Charles Edward set out on another rash and romantic expedition, for the old cause. He acted as regent for his father. He landed in Scotland in July, 1745, and was warmly welcomed by a few devoted Jacobites, who were ready to struggle and die, if need be, for the house of Stuart.

The prince was certainly not wanting in promptness. He at once caused his standard to be raised, and called on his countrymen, especially the Highlanders, to rally around their true prince. He marched rapidly from point lo point, and kindled a wild flame of enthusiasm as he went The Highlands resounded with loyal shouts, songs, and battle-cries, and the fierce mountaineers came rushing down from glens and forests and rocky fastnesses, in mad haste to offer themselves to "Royal Charlie." He received them all with gracious condescension, but he did not say or feel that they were doing anything more than simple duty in devoting to him their swords and their lives. He thought that all who acknowledged him as the rightful prince belonged to him, and he made as free with their blood and their money for his purposes, as with their wine and venison when they feasted him.

Success followed success, till all Scotland was roused and England in a terrible state of consternation. George the Second was now king. He, like his father, was little calculated to win the affection or admiration of his subjects. The con-trast between his majesty, who was a gross, dull man, and the elegant, handsome young Chevalier, was very great, and, for my part, I am afraid I should have gone with the Highlanders for " Bonnie Prince Charlie."

In September, the city of Edinburgh was taken by the Laird of Lochiel, the prince's greatest leader, when Charles Edward took possession of the Palace of Holyrood. Here he established a court, which, in spite of the times, became very gay and brilliant. The prince and his nobles were, however, soon called to sterner scenes. They met the English at Preston, and won a fa-mous victory. Their next undertaking was a march southward, with the bold purpose of driving King George from his own capital. But after reaching Derby, they were obliged to retreat, much to the rage and shame of the rash Chevalier. The next important event was the battle of Falkirk, which the prince won, but it did not advantage him much, for he was soon after it obliged to retire to the Highlands with his forces.

I have not space to relate the history of the rebellion from this to the great clos-ing battle of Culloden, which took place on the 16th of April, 1746. On this most terrible day, King George's forces, regular soldiers, were commanded by the Duke of Cumberland, and were 9,000 strong, opposed to only about 5,000 undisciplined Highlanders. Yet the prince's followers showed at first no signs of dismay at the odds against them. They shouted cheerily and sounded the wild *Pibroch* on their bagpipes, and rushed into battle with their old impetuosity. But they were met at all points with such steady, obstinate valor, and attacked with such overwhelming force, that they were soon disconcerted and driven back with dreadful loss. Some clans proved cowardly and treacherous, refusing to fight, and flying early from the field.

Though Prince Charles behaved gallantly enough while he had hope, he fled as fast and as far as any of them when he saw that the battle was lost. The Duke of Cumberland sent his dragoons in pursuit of the flying, commanding them to show no mercy, but to cut down all they could overtake. And they did it, — perhaps willingly, perhaps reluctantly; but the shame and crime of the inhuman slaughter rested, and always will rest, with the Duke himself. The flower of the Jacobite no-bility and gentry were slain in this battle, or executed for treason afterwards, and mourning and desolation were brought to thousands of happy Scottish homes.

It would take a volume to contain a faithful history of all Charles Edward's wanderings, perils, and adventures, from the day of his defeat at Culloden to that of his escape to Prance, five months after; for during all that time he was a hunted fugitive. Of course I cannot relate them here at length.

The prince first sought refuge in the west Highlands, where he met some of his adherents, whom he told, in his old, hopeful, undaunted way, that he intended to run over to France, for supplies and reinforcements, and return speedily to strike another blow for the good cause, — to settle the affairs of the Guelphs of Hanover. Some, as rash and sanguine as he, were comforted by these words ; but some sighed and shook their heads; none reproached him, except it was by the blood of their wounds, yet unwashed from their torn garments, and the deep despair in their eyes.

Prince Charles next embarked for the Long Island, near the Isle of Skye, on the western coast of Scotland, where he hoped to find some sort of a vessel to take him to France. He landed at South Uist, where he was met by Clanranald, a faithful follower, who, for safety, procured him a humble lodging in a forester's hut. But even here he was not Jong secure. General Campbell, the MacDonalds of Skye, MacLeod of MacLeod, and other Scots to the number of two thousand, who might have been in better business than hunting their true prince, came down upon the island, and eagerly searched it from north to south and east to west. It was at this time that Prince Charles met with his most romantic adventure. It happened that a beautiful young lady, Miss Flora MacDonald, was once on a visit to the Clanranalds of South Uist, and, hearing of the Chevalier's peril, nobly undertook to rescue him. Her stepfather . was in command of the MacDonalds, then on the island in search of him, and all her clan were anti-Jacobites; but few Scottish women were in heart ever opposed to the gallant young prince, and Mora's heart was now greatly touched by his misfortunes. She was not long in laying her plans, nor slow in carrying them out. She applied to her stepfather for a pass for herself, a man-servant, and a maid-servant, proposing to return to the Isle of Skye. She obtained the passport without difficulty, — Charles Edward disguising himself, and passing for the maidservant. Only think of it,—the splendid Chevalier assuming the dress and manner of a poor Scotch lass, and adding to his other appellations and titles the name of Betty Burke!

But elegant as the prince was in his own dress, he was ungraceful enough in this. Indeed, he came very near betraying himself many times by his awkwardness. He would every now and then strike into a grand princely stride, and, when reminded of it, would curb himself down into little mincing steps that everybody laughed to see. He did not seem to know just what to do with his hands; and when he sat down he was afraid to get up, lest he should entangle his feet in his skirts. He did not dare to trust his voice; so he concluded to say nothing to any one, which, of course, excited suspicions that he was not a woman. Yes, there were those who suspected Miss Betty Burke to be no better than a Stuart in disguise; but if they were tempted to betray their prince, and so win the reward, there was something in Mora Mac-Donald's eye which made them afraid and ashamed to commit such a treacherous act. So the party all got safely to the Isle of Skye. But the prince was not yet in security, though hidden in a dark cave by the wild sea-shore. Sir Alexander MacDonald was making a rigid search over the island. In this extremity, Flora did what many men would call a very rash thing, — confided her secret to another woman, and that woman the wife of Sir Alexander. Lady Margaret was frightened ; but she was generous and true, and never once thought of betraying the unfortunate prince to her husband. She concluded to confide the fugitive to the care of MacDonald of Kingsburg. Flora accompanied her charge to the house of this MacDonald, who received him respectfully and promised him his protection; not only because he was his prince, but a fellow-man in deadly peril; and not from fear, but love of Flora Mao-Donald, who had captivated him by her generous heroism.

From Kingsburg the prince went to the island of Rasa, where he suffered great privations, and from thence back to Scotland, where he wandered and wandered, in want and weariness and peril, — everywhere hunted, but everywhere finding friends, who, though poor and wretched like himself, were too proud and noble to win wealth by betraying him to his enemies. For several weeks, he took refuge in a cavern with seven other outlaws, who had taken to robbing " as the only way of gaining an honest livelihood," they said. Prince Charles was in no condition to be overscrupulous, so he allowed them to procure him a change of clothes from the first well-dressed traveller they could waylay, and ate and drank what they set before him, "asking no questions for conscience' sake."

Charles Edward owed his final escape to a singular piece of devotion and fore-thought. There was a young officer of his army who was said to look remarkably like him, — one Roderick Mac-Kinzie, now a fugitive like himself, who was one day overtaken by the King's troops, and mortally wounded. As he lay in his last agonies, he looked up at his murderers and exclaimed, " Ah, villains, you have slain your prince !" This was a falsehood certainly, but there was something so noble about it that one can hardly condemn it,— at all events, it saved the prince's life, for Roderick's words were believed, and his head was taken off and sent to London. Here the mistake was discovered; but in the mean time, the search for the prince was given over in Scotland, and he had time to make his escape. He sailed for France from Lochnannah with Lochiel and about an hundred others, on the 15th of September, and landed at Morlaix on the 29th; and so ended the last attempt of the Stuarts to regain the throne of their ancestors. Not that they ever wholly abandoned their pretensions and their plans,— they clung to them desperately for a long time. But they no longer found many others mad enough to sacrifice their all for a cause so hopeless. And the world went on, — the scaffold ceased to drip with the blood of their followers, and the prison to echo their groans. The grass sprang up long and rank on the battle-field of Culloden, — over the ashes of homes desolated in their wars, over the graves of men who had died broken-hearted for their sakes, of mothers and wives made childless and widowed by their ambition, — the pibroch was sounded no longer among the wild Highlands, — the fiery cross was borne no more from house to house, a portent of battle and death, — and the Stuarts were forgotten.

Once, as I was strolling about a damp, mouldy old church in Frascati, a little town among the Alban hills, near Rome, I suddenly came upon a marble slab in the wall, with a Latin inscription, which said that under it was buried ***Charles Edward, King of England, Scotland, and Ireland***. So here he lay, the gallant prince, the accomplished chevalier, the darling royal Charlie of the Scots.

He died at Rome in 1788, but it seems was buried here, in his brother's cathedral, though there is a great Stuart monument in St. Peter's Church. The latter part of his life was unhappy and discreditable. It seems it would have been better if he had fallen in his noblest days on his last battle-field, and been buried there. There his royal blood might at least have nourished a daisy or a wild lily, and his memory would have haunted the spot like the pure air and the sunshine. Here is no light, no freshness, nothing but shadow and mould, and that pompous Latin epitaph, claiming for his poor dust the crown he vainly grasped after all his life.

Now a few words about Flora MacDonald. After the escape of Charles Edward, she and her brave lover were arrested and imprisoned in the Tower; but the king was soon obliged from very shame to pardon and release them. Then Mora became, as they say, "all the rage" in London. Everybody crowded to see her, honored and applauded her. Even the king's eldest son, Prince Frederick, praised her generous heroism. Perhaps he thought in such revolutionary times, he might need such loyal devotion as well as the *other* Prince of Wales, and believed in encouraging such things.

The gifts bestowed upon Flora by her numerous admirers amounted to no less than fifteen hundred pounds, — quite a little fortune, which she bestowed upon MacDonald of Kingsburg, with what was infinitely more precious, her love and her hand in marriage. These two noble Mac-Donalds resided for a while in America, but they returned to pass their last years in the Isle of Skye. Their graves are in the churchyard of Kilmuir. The tombstone of the heroine was once inlaid with a marble slab, but this has been broken and carried off bit by bit, by curious tourists. Yet she did not need it; her beautiful fame is better than a hundred epitaphs. Flora Mac-Donald, the fairest flower that ever bloomed in the rough path of her prince's hard fortunes, giving a tender grace to his tragic story, and sweetening his memory in the heart of the world.

Melrose. - Abbotsford. - Dryburgh.

# SIR WALTER SCOTT.

IT was on a cool and breezy autumn morning, now sunny, and now showery, that we bade adieu to dear old Edinburgh, and turned our faces towards England, intending to visit a few remarkable places on our way. We stopped first at Melrose, to see the ruined Abbey which Sir Walter Scott has made famous by his " Lay of the Last Minstrel."

Melrose, about thirty-seven miles from Edinburgh, is situated on the Tweed, a small but beautiful river, and above it rise the gray Eildon Hills, long famed in song and story. The Abbey, the most magnificent and perfect specimen of Gothic architecture existing in Scotland, was founded in 1136 by David the First, was destroyed by Edward the Second, and rebuilt by Robert Bruce. It was afterwards greatly injured at various times by the English, but finally made a complete ruin of by the Protestants, at the Reformation. Yet there is enough of it still remaining to give one an imposing idea of its beauty and grandeur. Its sculpture is still wonderful to see, and the ivy and wall-flowers which grow all about among the ruins are not more perfect and graceful than the stone vines, flowers, and foliage in the windows and arches, and around the mighty pillars,— carved so many hundred years ago.

A host of noble knights, and a king or two, have been buried in Melrose Abbey. Many of the warlike family of Douglas sleep the long sleep in this desolate but lovely place. Robert Bruce's heart, which travelled so far and went through so many adventures after it was out of his body, was at last deposited here under the high altar, where it long ago mingled with common dust. But his noble fame yet lives, and beats on, like a brave, strong heart, in the life of his country.

As I was standing opposite one of the great windows of the Abbey, admiring its exquisite sculptures, the old guide, pointing to a fallen pillar, said, " That, madam, was the favorite seat o' Sir Walter Scott. Mony 's the time I hae seen him sitting there, leaning on his staff, wi' his dogs at his feet, and the great thoughts glissting and glowering in his een."

I sat down on this pillar for a moment, with more reverence than I had felt a few months before, while sitting in Westminster Abbey on the " Stone of Scone," on which so many Scottish and English monarchs had been crowned.

From Melrose we drove a few miles to Abbots-ford, the seat of Sir Walter Scott. This is one of the most noble and beautiful residences in all Scotland. It is situated on the south bank of the Tweed, near its junction with the Gala, sur-rounded by a fine picturesque country, and in full sight of the Eildon Hills.

The delightful grounds of Abbotsford are now as they were planned and plant-ed by Sir Walter. The house is of the Gothic style, with a great many towers and gables, irregular and peculiar, but very stately and beautiful.

We entered by a handsome porch, ornamented with petrified stag-horns, into a lofty hall, paved with black and white marble, brought from the Hebrides, and panelled with richly carved oak, from the old royal palace of Dumfermline. The walls are hung with ancient arms, and decorated with the armorial crests of the great Scottish families of the borders. From this we passed into the armory, where, among many curious specimens of arms, we saw Montrose's sword and Rob Roy's gun, — two of Sir Walter's greatest treasures.

At one end of the armory is the drawing-room, a very elegant apartment, lined with cedar-wood, and furnished with ebony, and containing several curious and costly carved cabinets. At the other end is the dining-room, a spacious and lofty sa-loon, with a ceiling of black oak. Here Sir Walter entertained not only his many friends, but countless strangers and foreign travellers, with a hospitality like that of the great-hearted barons of old. This room contains several fine pictures, and interesting family portraits; among the latter is a likeness of Sir Walter when he was a little boy. It represents a delicate, fair-haired child; but the expression is very thoughtful and earnest, and the head has a grand, prophetic look about it.

The next room I recollect is a charming little breakfast parlor, looking out upon the Tweed, and the hills of Ettrick and Yarrow. Then there is the library, the larg-est room in the house. It has a roof of oak, carved after beautiful models in Roslin Castle. The collection of books is a very rare one, and amounts to twenty thousand volumes. Out of the library opens the study, — a small, neat apartment, containing a few books, and furnished only with a plain writing-table and an arm-chair. Here Sir Walter used to write.

In a small closet, opening out of the study, are kept the clothes which Sir Walter last wore about the grounds of Abbotsford. It is a very plain country-suit, — a dark-blue coat, with large buttons, plaid trousers, a pair of thick shoes, a broad-brimmed hat, and a sturdy walking-stick. The sight of these, more than anything else in that house, touched my heart. No costly royal robes, glittering with diamonds and pearls, could ever seem to me so worthy of reverence as these plain, homely garments, on which must have fallen many tears of tender love and sorrow, worth more than all the jewels in the world.

We went away from Abbotsford very thoughtful and sad, and did not say much to each other throughout our drive to Dryburgh Abbey. Here, in a lovely, lonely spot, in the midst of a noble old ruin, overgrown with ivy, wall-flowers, and sweet wild-roses, Sir Walter was buried beside his dear wife, — and here since his eldest son has been laid.

Sir Walter loved to visit this beautiful ruin, which was once the property of his ancestors, and it seems a fitting and grand place for him to rest in, after all the toils, cares, and sorrows of his hard, though splendid life.

I think, dear children, that I cannot make a better close to this volume of sketches and recollections of Scotland, than by relating a true and wonderful, though perhaps you will think rather a sad story: —

# THE LIFE OF SIR WALTER SCOTT.

"Walter Scott, the son of Walter Scott, was born in Edinburgh, in 1771. His father, a lawyer of some repute, who belonged to an old and highly respectable family, was a man of good mind and excellent heart; his mother, the daughter of an eminent physician, was an amiable and intellectual lady.

Mr. and Mrs. Scott had twelve children, but all, except four sons and one daughter, died in infancy. Walter was one of the youngest. He was a strong and healthy child, till he was about eighteen months old, when, after a little attack of fever, resulting from teething, he lost the use of his right leg.

The best physicians of Edinburgh were called to see him, and everything which they believed or imagined could help him was done; but all in vain. At last, the doctors gave up,—just in time to save his life, probably, and he was sent to his grandfather Scott's, for the benefit of country air. Here he remained for several years, most kindly and tenderly cared for, and improving in health and strength, but not wholly recovering from his lameness. Indeed, he suffered from it, more or less, to the day of his death.

There was an old shepherd on his grandfather's farm of whom little Walter was very fond. This man, "Auld Sandy Ormistoun," used to take him on his shoulders, and carry him out to the hills where he was watching his flocks. Here the child would roll about on the soft, green turf, among the sheep and lambs, and watch the white fleecy clouds floating above him, — thinking, perhaps, that they looked like another flock of sheep, in the great fields of the sky, — and be quiet and good and happy, hour after hour. One day the shepherd left him alone, and went down to the house for something, and while he was gone a thunder-storm came up. Then his Aunt Jenny, remembering where he was, ran to the hills to bring him home. She expected to find him dreadfully frightened; but he was lying on his back, looking up at the flashes of lightning, and exclaiming: " Bonnie! bonnie !"

When Walter was about six years old, he was taken to Bath, England, for the benefit of the waters; which, however, did not do him much good. While here, he saw, for the first time, a play acted. There was a scene in this which represented a quarrel between two brothers, and the affectionate little fellow was so much shocked at it, that he cried out indignantly: " Ain't they **brothers** ? "

On returning from Bath, Walter, after a little visit to his home, went back to his grandfather's, where he throve best. He was mostly under the care of his

Aunt Jenny, a good and beautiful woman, but his grandparents and his kind Uncle Thomas were very fond of him. His grandfather used to tell him stories, and his grandmother would repeat ballads to him, and almost as soon as he could talk, he showed a remarkable fondness for such things.

By degrees, he grew strong enough to walk, then to run and climb among the rocks and crags. At last, he got quite above riding old Sandy Or-mistoun, but learned to canter about on a Shetland pony, no larger than a Newfoundland dog. Indeed, she was so small that he used to ride her into the house. He fed her with his own hands, and called her " Marion."

But though he grew to be a merry, sturdy, manly boy, Walter was always gentle and good. As one of the old servants said, long afterwards : " He was a sweet-tempered bairn; a darling with all the house."

When he was about eight years old, he returned home to live and go to school. He was not considered one of the first scholars in the institution he attended, — the Edinburgh High School, for he lacked ambition and diligence, — but he was always thought a remarkably able and quickwitted boy. His memory was really wonderful. There was no end to the songs, ballads, and fairy tales which he had by heart. If anything struck his fancy, he could remember it without difficulty. His father rather discouraged his passion for po-etry and romance, but his mother, who was also poetic in her tastes, used to read with him, and listen to his fine recitations with delight. He was greatly beloved by his schoolmates, who eagerly crowded around him in play hours, to listen to his stories, and who were sure of his help and sympathy in all their boyish difficulties and sorrows.

He did not study as assiduously as he should have done, and he afterwards regretted this ; but he read constantly, and so laid up, in his own irregular way, a vast store of information. He could not be brought to love Greek and Latin, but he learned to read, mostly by himself, German, Spanish, and Italian, and he spoke French very well. He never let his lameness and awkward limp keep him from exercising with the other boys, and after a while he distinguished himself by feats of strength and daring. He grew tall and robust, and used to take long walks into the country, with his favorite schoolfellows, sometimes taking an arm of one of them, and always making use of a cane.

At sixteen, he entered upon an apprenticeship to his father. He was faithful and diligent in business, but he still found time for reading and the manly sports in which he had such delight. During this apprenticeship he made several excursions into the Highlands, on business, and there acquired much information, which he afterwards made excellent use of. Indeed, wherever he went, through all his life, from everything he saw and heard, he learned something useful.

There are many interesting anecdotes told of Walter Scott in his youth, but I have room for only one, which seems to me very beautiful.

One winter, while attending the lectures of the celebrated Dugald Stewart, upon Moral Philosophy, he used to sit beside a young man who seemed in humble circumstances, but who had an interesting and modest manner, and was evidently a diligent student. Scott liked him, and of course he liked Scott, — everybody did. Yet, though they became quite familiar friends, and often had long walks, and frank, cordial talks together, Walter noticed that his companion never said anything about his own home, or parentage. One day, as Scott was returning alone from a ramble, he was struck by the venerable appearance of a "**Bluegown**" a beggar of the most respectable class, who was standing by the way-side, leaning on his staff, and silently holding out his hat for alms. Scott gave him some money, and passed on. Several times after he found him in the same place and gave him alms, and once this happened when he was walking with the poor student. As he dropped his gift into the extended hat, he noticed a strange expression on the young man's face, and, as they went on, he asked: " Do you know anything to the old man's discredit, Willie ? "

His friend burst into tears, as he answered: " O no, God forbid, but I am a poor wretch to be ashamed to speak to him,— *he is my own father*! He has enough laid by to serve him for his own old days, but he stands bleaching his head in the wind, that he may get the means to pay for my education."

Scott felt deeply for the poor fellow's mortifying situation; he soothed him, comforted him, kept his secret, and never once thought of dropping his acquaintance. He was too noble for that. If he had not been, I should not now be writing his life with so much love in my heart.

Some time after, when the lectures were over, Walter one day met the old "Bluegown," who, looking all round to see that nobody could overhear him, said: "I find, sir, that you have been very kind to my Willie. He had often spoken of it before I saw you together. Will you pardon such a liberty, and give me the honor of seeing you under my poor roof? Willie has not been well, and it would do him good to see your face."

Of course, Scott went. He found his humble friends living in a neat little cabin at St. Leon-ard's, near Edinburgh. Willie, very pale and thin, from his illness, was sitting on a stone bench by the door, looking for his coming, and was very glad and grateful when he saw him. During this visit, the old man talked of his plans and hopes for his darling son, and said: "Please God, I may live to see my bairn wag his head in a pulpit yet."

When Scott returned home, he confided the story of Willie to his mother, and so much interested her in him that she exerted her influence and obtained for him the situation of tutor in a gentleman's family, after which his poor old father gave up begging and lived upon his savings.

So when Willie came to "wag his head in a pulpit," he had to thank the friendship of his fellow-student, then a great man. I hope he did not boast of him in public, but remembered him when he prayed alone.

When Walter Scott was about twenty-eight, an advocate of some distinction, and just becoming known as a poet, he visited the English lakes, and while stopping at Gilsland, he one morning saw a beautiful young lady on horseback. He was charmed both by her sweet face and her graceful riding, — he made her acquaintance, and liked her so well, that as soon as he could win her love, he married her. So Miss Charlotte Margaret Carpenter became Mrs. Walter Scott, to the satisfaction of all his friends. At this time, the poet is described as tall and handsome, with a glowing, kindly, honest face,—now playful as a child's, now thoughtful and dreamy, but always sweet and gentle. He had an intense love for everything beautiful, high, and honorable, and a manly scorn of meanness, pretension, and coarseness. He had no vices, no follies, and no enemies. He was sincere, simple, and courteous to all; and, great as his intellect was, his heart was still greater.

Shortly after his marriage, Scott was appointed Sheriff of Selkirkshire, and some years later, Clerk of Session, — offices which he long filled with faithfulness and honor. He was thirty-four when he published his first long poem, " *The Lay of the Last Minstrel*" which at once made him a famous man. He was then living in a beautiful country-place, called Ashestiel, and had four children, — Sophia, Walter, Anne, and Charles. He never had any more, but God in his goodness spared all these till he was gone, and then let them follow him soon. Walter Scott was a careful and tender father. He loved the society of his children, and was never disturbed by their play and prattle. They sat at the same table with him, walked and rode with him, and came into his study at all times. He talked with them, told them stories and ballads, taught them to be truthful and courageous, and took part in all their pleasures and sorrows. And the children, though they deeply honored and loved " papa," did not fear him, or have any uncomfortable awe in his presence. In the dreariest weather, they were content and merry if he were at home, and they could not enjoy the pleasantest excursion, if he were not along.

It was said of Scott, that "he was a gentleman, even to his dogs." He was more, — a merciful Christian man to all dumb creatures. On Sunday he would not use his horses, for, he said, " they also needed a day of rest," but after church service, he would walk out with his family and his dogs, and, when the weather would allow, dine with them in the open air. At these times he gave his children religious instruction, and told them Bible stories in such a simple, pleasant way, as to make them think Sunday the happiest day of the week.

There were always several fine dogs in Walter Scott's family, who were pets and playfellows for the children, and almost companions for their master. The most famous of them were Camp, a terrier, and Maida, a stag-hound. These two were several times painted, by great artists. Maida grew so tired of being " taken," at last, that as soon as she saw any one preparing to make a sketch of her, she would get up and walk off in disgust.

Camp always accompanied his master in his rides and rambles, till he got too old and feeble, —but he never lost his affection or his intelligence. At Ashestiel he would go out every night to meet Scott, always taking the way indicated by the servant, who would say to him: " Camp, the Sheriff is coming home by the ford," or, " by the hill."

Shortly after the family removed to Edinburgh, Camp died, and was buried by moonlight, in a little garden, back of the house, and in sight of the window of his master's study. The poet him-self laid him in the grave, and sadly smoothed down the turf above him, while the whole family stood by in tears. Scott had engaged to dine out that day, but excused himself on account " of the death of a dear old friend." How I like that in him!

Maida, beautiful Maida ! lived and died at Abbotsford, where a monument was erected to her memory.

In 1808 and 1810, Scott published " Mar-mion " and " The Lady of the Lake," delightful poems, which made him idolized in his native land, and spread the circle of his fame till it had widened over the world. Soon after this, he purchased Ab-botsford, then a lonely, uncultivated place, but which he saw could be made very beautiful. His first plan was to build a simple cottage; but, as his means increased, he became ambitious for something grander, and, after several years, the present noble mansion was erected.

In 1814, Scott published " Waverley," the first of the most wonderful series of romances ever written, called the " The Waverley Novels." He did not give his name as the writer of this work; and for several years only his publishers and a few friends knew to a certainty that he was the sole author of this and the many splendid novels that rapidly followed it.

For a few bright years, Scott was one of the happiest as well as one of the greatest of men. His works brought him in large sums of money, which he spent in buying new lands, in planting and building at Abbotsford. He was successful in all he undertook. Men and women of genius, princes, and the highest nobility flocked to see him. He was rich, he was honored, and, what was far better, he saw his beautiful children growing up around him, healthful, intelligent, and good. I am glad to be able to say that he bore his fame and fortune with a manly humility, and always found his greatest happiness in helping and pleasing others.

Scott had two friends at Abbotsford whom he especially loved and trusted, — Mr. Laidlaw, or " Willie Laidlaw," his steward, a very intelligent man, and a poet; and Tom Purdie, his forester, the most faithful of servants, who loved his master with all his great, honest heart.

I hare only space to mention a few of the principal events in the busy and splendid life of Scott. He was made a baronet by George the Fourth, in 1820. Shortly after, his eldest daughter, Sophia, was married to Mr. Lockhart. His son "Walter was in the army; Charles was a clerk in government office.

And now I come to the dark days. In consequence of some unwise speculations, his publishers, with whom he was in partnership, in a time of commercial difficulty and panic, became involved, failed, and Sir Walter was ruined!

He gave up all to his creditors, even his beloved books; and nobly resolved to devote the rest of his life, if necessary, to the payment of all demands against him, enormous as they were.

About this time, trouble after trouble came upon him. His little grandson, John Hugh Lockhart, or "Hugh Littlejohn," as he is called in the " Tales of a Grandfather," for whom, on account of a lameness like his own, he had always felt a peculiar tenderness, was given over by the physicians as an incurable invalid.

Then Lady Scott, his gentle and beloved wife, died at Abbotsford, after a painful illness. Yet, amid losses, embarrassments, anxieties, and bitter griefs, the brave and conscientious man labored on, allowing himself no time for rest or weeping. He finished his great "Life of Napoleon," — he wrote novels, essays, reviews, biographies, poems, toiling so incessantly, so *terribly* hard, that at length his health, and, what was sadder still, his mind, began to give way. Within the first two years after his failure, he paid his creditors forty thousand pounds! — all made by his pen.

One evening, in 1829, " honest Tom Purdie," after a hard day's work, leaned his head on his table and fell asleep. As he had seemed perfectly well, his family did not try to wake him for some time, but went softly about, and spoke low, for they knew he was tired. When supper wag ready, they called him. He did not answer. They lifted his head from the table, and found that he was dead! This was another shock to the affectionate heart and broken spirit of Sir Walter.

A few months after, he had a paralytic stroke, —was extremely ill and speechless for some time, but rallied, and very soon went to work again. It was in vain his children and friends entreated him to give himself a little rest. He could not rest, he said, he could not live under such a load of debt. In 1830, he had another attack of paralysis, yet rallied again, and that same year paid his creditors another large sum. They, in gratitude for his exertions, gave back to him the library, museum, plate, furniture, and paintings at Abbotsford,—where he was allowed to reside when he wished. This generous kindness cheered him very much, and he went on with his labors. But alas, he could not write any more in his old strong, clear style! There seemed a mist over his mind, and his thoughts grew weak and wandering. Yet, every now and then, his genius flashed out as bright as ever, and as his daily talk and habits were little changed, those around him hardly dared to say to one another, " He is failing."

In the spring of 1831, he had a stroke of paralysis which not only injured his memory and his speech, but somewhat distorted his face. He also suffered greatly from rheumatism, Cramps, and increased lameness. From every attack he rose up feebler, and more bewildered, but still strong in will. He was like some noble animal, struck down by repeated blows, but still struggling up and staggering on, weak and blinded. In the fall, he went to Italy, with a little hope of getting better. He was accompanied by his son Walter and his daughter Anne. They visited many places which would have deeply interested the poet in his happier days,—but now they gave him little pleasure. He was ill, weary, melancholy, and homesick. His great fame was now a real affliction, for it caused people to press upon him in a way that was almost cruel. His chief comfort was in a strange delusion. He imagined that all his debts were paid, and he was a free man, with ample means once more. At times, this happy hallucination left him, and he would go to work harder than ever, and bring on another attack. While at Naples, he wrote in his diary: "Poor Johnny Lockhart! The boy is gone whom we made so much of." Yes, his darling grandson was dead.

Sir Walter grew alarmingly worse, and begged to be taken home, that he might die at Abbots-ford ; so, early in the summer his party returned to England. At the hotel in London he lay for some weeks in a state of utter exhaustion and stupor. Yet he knew his children, and would rouse up now and then and speak to them in the old loving way, and tell them how his heart yearned for Abbotsford. As soon as it was thought safe for him to travel farther, he was taken home. He did not seem to take notice of anything till they came in sight of Melrose, and other familiar places, when he became greatly excited with joy, and as they drew near Abbots-ford he could scarcely be kept in the carriage, he was so impatient to reach it.

Mr. Laidlaw met him at the porch, and helped him into the house. Sir Walter's eye lighted up at sight of his old friend, and he exclaimed, " Ha! Willie Laidlaw, 0 man, how often I have thought of you." His dogs came crowding around his chair, fawning on him and licking his hands. He bent down and smiled and wept over them for a while, then fell back and went to sleep.

The next morning he awoke refreshed, calm and conscious, and asked to be taken out to see his garden and grounds. Willie Laidlaw wheeled him about for some time, in a Bath chair, followed by his children, his grandchildren, and his favorite dogs. He often smiled tenderly on them all, and on the summer glory of the flowers and trees, and talked a little, very sweetly and like himself. Then he wished to be wheeled through his house, and as they passed around the lofty suite of rooms, endeared to him by so many sweet and bright memories, he said," I have seen much, but nothing like my own house, — give me one turn more."

After this, for a little while, he took the air daily in his Bath chair, and so visited several spots most dear to him in his grounds. He often asked Mr. Lockhart to read to him, and it was noticed that, though he seemed to have forgotten poems that he had once had by heart, he never forgot the **Bible**, which he loved more than ever; and one night, when his little grandson, Walter Lockhart, was repeating some of Watts's Hymns, he seemed to remember them perfectly.

One day, he asked to be taken to his study, for he wanted to write. His daughters opened his desk and got everything ready for him, and he was wheeled into his old place. He smiled and said, "Thank you, — now give me my pen and leave me to myself for a while." Mrs. Lockhart put the pen into his hand, but the poor old man could not hold it. As it dropped upon the paper he sank back on his pillow, burst into tears, and gave up forever!

Soon after this, he was taken to his own room, which he never left again. Yet he lingered until the 21st of September, most of the time in a state of complete stupor and unconsciousness. On the morning of the 17th he awoke conscious and composed. He seemed to think himself dying, and said to Mr. Lockhart: " I may have but a minute to speak to you. My dear, be a good man, — be virtuous, — be religious, — be *a good man*. Nothing else, will give you any comfort when you come to lie here."

Mr. Lockhart asked if he should call Sophia and Anne (Sir Walter's sons had been obliged to return to their posts). " No," he said, " don't disturb them. Poor souls ! I know they were up all night. God bless you all."

These were his last audible words. He sunk again into a deep stupor, and only revived for a moment when his sons came to him. He knew them, and blessed them with his eyes.

He passed away very calmly, with all his children kneeling around him, and his son Walter kissed down his eyelids for the last sleep.

When, a few days after, that bereaved family returned from Dryburgh Abbey, where they had laid the worn and aged form of their beloved, to beautiful and desolate Abbotsford, they tried to comfort one another with thoughts of him in a better home, — in the midst of all his loved ones gone before, — with his tender wife by his side, and dear little Johnny at his knee.

When her idolized father was gone, Anne Scott had no heart to stay. She drooped and died within that year. Sophia followed a few years after, and Walter and Charles have since died. Abbotsford is now occupied by Mr. Hope, who married a granddaughter of Sir Walter Scott.

THE END.

### The Codes Of Hammurabi And Moses
### W. W. Davies

QTY

The discovery of the Hammurabi Code is one of the greatest achievements of archaeology, and is of paramount interest, not only to the student of the Bible, but also to all those interested in ancient history...

**Religion**     ISBN: *1-59462-338-4*     **Pages:132**

*MSRP $12.95*

### The Theory of Moral Sentiments
### Adam Smith

QTY

This work from 1749. contains original theories of conscience amd moral judgment and it is the foundation for systemof morals.

**Philosophy**  ISBN: *1-59462-777-0*     **Pages:536**

*MSRP $19.95*

### Jessica's First Prayer
### Hesba Stretton

QTY

In a screened and secluded corner of one of the many railway-bridges which span the streets of London there could be seen a few years ago, from five o'clock every morning until half past eight, a tidily set-out coffee-stall, consisting of a trestle and board, upon which stood two large tin cans, with a small fire of charcoal burning under each so as to keep the coffee boiling during the early hours of the morning when the work-people were thronging into the city on their way to their daily toil...

**Pages:84**

**Childrens**    ISBN: *1-59462-373-2*     *MSRP $9.95*

### My Life and Work
### Henry Ford

QTY

Henry Ford revolutionized the world with his implementation of mass production for the Model T automobile. Gain valuable business insight into his life and work with his own auto-biography... "We have only started on our development of our country we have not as yet, with all our talk of wonderful progress, done more than scratch the surface. The progress has been wonderful enough but..."

**Pages:300**

**Biographies/**   ISBN: *1-59462-198-5*     *MSRP $21.95*

## The Art of Cross-Examination
## Francis Wellman

QTY

I presume it is the experience of every author, after his first book is published upon an important subject, to be almost overwhelmed with a wealth of ideas and illustrations which could readily have been included in his book, and which to his own mind, at least, seem to make a second edition inevitable. Such certainly was the case with me; and when the first edition had reached its sixth impression in five months, I rejoiced to learn that it seemed to my publishers that the book had met with a sufficiently favorable reception to justify a second and considerably enlarged edition. ..

**Pages:412**

Reference    **ISBN:** *1-59462-647-2*    *MSRP $19.95*

## On the Duty of Civil Disobedience
## Henry David Thoreau

QTY

Thoreau wrote his famous essay, On the Duty of Civil Disobedience, as a protest against an unjust but popular war and the immoral but popular institution of slave-owning. He did more than write—he declined to pay his taxes, and was hauled off to gaol in consequence. Who can say how much this refusal of his hastened the end of the war and of slavery ?

Law    **ISBN:** *1-59462-747-9*    **Pages:48**

*MSRP $7.45*

## Dream Psychology Psychoanalysis for Beginners
## Sigmund Freud

QTY

Sigmund Freud, born Sigismund Schlomo Freud (May 6, 1856 - September 23, 1939), was a Jewish-Austrian neurologist and psychiatrist who co-founded the psychoanalytic school of psychology. Freud is best known for his theories of the unconscious mind, especially involving the mechanism of repression; his redefinition of sexual desire as mobile and directed towards a wide variety of objects; and his therapeutic techniques, especially his understanding of transference in the therapeutic relationship and the presumed value of dreams as sources of insight into unconscious desires.

**Pages:196**

Psychology    **ISBN:** *1-59462-905-6*    *MSRP $15.45*

## The Miracle of Right Thought
## Orison Swett Marden

QTY

Believe with all of your heart that you will do what you were made to do. When the mind has once formed the habit of holding cheerful, happy, prosperous pictures, it will not be easy to form the opposite habit. It does not matter how improbable or how far away this realization may see, or how dark the prospects may be, if we visualize them as best we can, as vividly as possible, hold tenaciously to them and vigorously struggle to attain them, they will gradually become actualized, realized in the life. But a desire, a longing without endeavor, a yearning abandoned or held indifferently will vanish without realization.

**Pages:360**

Self Help    **ISBN:** *1-59462-644-8*    *MSRP $25.45*

**The Rosicrucian Cosmo-Conception Mystic Christianity** *by Max Heindel*    ISBN: *1-59462-188-8*  **$38.95**
*The Rosicrucian Cosmo-conception is not dogmatic, neither does it appeal to any other authority than the reason of the student. It is: not controversial, but is: sent forth in the, hope that it may help to clear...*    New Age/Religion Pages 646

**Abandonment To Divine Providence** *by Jean-Pierre de Caussade*    ISBN: *1-59462-228-0*  **$25.95**
*"The Rev. Jean Pierre de Caussade was one of the most remarkable spiritual writers of the Society of Jesus in France in the 18th Century. His death took place at Toulouse in 1751. His works have gone through many editions and have been republished...*    Inspirational/Religion Pages 400

**Mental Chemistry** *by Charles Haanel*    ISBN: *1-59462-192-6*  **$23.95**
*Mental Chemistry allows the change of material conditions by combining and appropriately utilizing the power of the mind. Much like applied chemistry creates something new and unique out of careful combinations of chemicals the mastery of mental chemistry...*    New Age Pages 354

**The Letters of Robert Browning and Elizabeth Barret Barrett 1845-1846 vol II**    ISBN: *1-59462-193-4*  **$35.95**
*by Robert Browning and Elizabeth Barrett*    Biographies Pages 596

**Gleanings In Genesis (volume I)** *by Arthur W. Pink*    ISBN: *1-59462-130-6*  **$27.45**
*Appropriately has Genesis been termed "the seed plot of the Bible" for in it we have, in germ form, almost all of the great doctrines which are afterwards fully developed in the books of Scripture which follow...*    Religion/Inspirational Pages 420

**The Master Key** *by L. W. de Laurence*    ISBN: *1-59462-001-6*  **$30.95**
*In no branch of human knowledge has there been a more lively increase of the spirit of research during the past few years than in the study of Psychology, Concentration and Mental Discipline. The requests for authentic lessons in Thought Control, Mental Discipline and...*    New Age/Business Pages 422

**The Lesser Key Of Solomon Goetia** *by L. W. de Laurence*    ISBN: *1-59462-092-X*  **$9.95**
*This translation of the first book of the "Lernegton" which is now for the first time made accessible to students of Talismanic Magic was done, after careful collation and edition, from numerous Ancient Manuscripts in Hebrew, Latin, and French...*    New Age/Occult Pages 92

**Rubaiyat Of Omar Khayyam** *by Edward Fitzgerald*    ISBN:*1-59462-332-5*  **$13.95**
*Edward Fitzgerald, whom the world has already learned, in spite of his own efforts to remain within the shadow of anonymity, to look upon as one of the rarest poets of the century, was born at Bredfield, in Suffolk, on the 31st of March, 1809. He was the third son of John Purcell...*    Music Pages 172

**Ancient Law** *by Henry Maine*    ISBN: *1-59462-128-4*  **$29.95**
*The chief object of the following pages is to indicate some of the earliest ideas of mankind, as they are reflected in Ancient Law, and to point out the relation of those ideas to modern thought.*    Religion/History Pages 452

**Far-Away Stories** *by William J. Locke*    ISBN: *1-59462-129-2*  **$19.45**
*"Good wine needs no bush, but a collection of mixed vintages does. And this book is just such a collection. Some of the stories I do not want to remain buried for ever in the museum files of dead magazine-numbers an author's not unpardonable vanity..."*    Fiction Pages 272

**Life of David Crockett** *by David Crockett*    ISBN: *1-59462-250-7*  **$27.45**
*"Colonel David Crockett was one of the most remarkable men of the times in which he lived. Born in humble life, but gifted with a strong will, an indomitable courage, and unremitting perseverance...*    Biographies/New Age Pages 424

**Lip-Reading** *by Edward Nitchie*    ISBN: *1-59462-206-X*  **$25.95**
*Edward B. Nitchie, founder of the New York School for the Hard of Hearing, now the Nitchie School of Lip-Reading, Inc, wrote "LIP-READING Principles and Practice". The development and perfecting of this meritorious work on lip-reading was an undertaking...*    How-to Pages 400

**A Handbook of Suggestive Therapeutics, Applied Hypnotism, Psychic Science**    ISBN: *1-59462-214-0*  **$24.95**
*by Henry Munro*    Health/New Age/Health/Self-help Pages 376

**A Doll's House: and Two Other Plays** *by Henrik Ibsen*    ISBN: *1-59462-112-8*  **$19.95**
*Henrik Ibsen created this classic when in revolutionary 1848 Rome. Introducing some striking concepts in playwriting for the realist genre, this play has been studied the world over.*    Fiction/Classics/Plays 308

**The Light of Asia** *by sir Edwin Arnold*    ISBN: *1-59462-204-3*  **$13.95**
*In this poetic masterpiece, Edwin Arnold describes the life and teachings of Buddha. The man who was to become known as Buddha to the world was born as Prince Gautama of India but he rejected the worldly riches and abandoned the reigns of power when...*    Religion/History/Biographies Pages 170

**The Complete Works of Guy de Maupassant** *by Guy de Maupassant*    ISBN: *1-59462-157-8*  **$16.95**
*"For days and days, nights and nights, I had dreamed of that first kiss which was to consecrate our engagement, and I knew not on what spot I should put my lips..."*    Fiction/Classics Pages 240

**The Art of Cross-Examination** *by Francis L. Wellman*    ISBN: *1-59462-309-0*  **$26.95**
*Written by a renowned trial lawyer, Wellman imparts his experience and uses case studies to explain how to use psychology to extract desired information through questioning.*    How-to/Science/Reference Pages 408

**Answered or Unanswered?** *by Louisa Vaughan*    ISBN: *1-59462-248-5*  **$10.95**
*Miracles of Faith in China*    Religion Pages 112

**The Edinburgh Lectures on Mental Science (1909)** *by Thomas*    ISBN: *1-59462-008-3*  **$11.95**
*This book contains the substance of a course of lectures recently given by the writer in the Queen Street Hall, Edinburgh. Its purpose is to indicate the Natural Principles governing the relation between Mental Action and Material Conditions...*    New Age/Psychology Pages 148

**Ayesha** *by H. Rider Haggard*    ISBN: *1-59462-301-5*  **$24.95**
*Verily and indeed it is the unexpected that happens! Probably if there was one person upon the earth from whom the Editor of this, and of a certain previous history, did not expect to hear again...*    Classics Pages 380

**Ayala's Angel** *by Anthony Trollope*    ISBN: *1-59462-352-X*  **$29.95**
*The two girls were both pretty, but Lucy who was twenty-one who supposed to be simple and comparatively unattractive, whereas Ayala was credited, as her Bombwhat romantic name might show, with poetic charm and a taste for romance. Ayala when her father died was nineteen...*    Fiction Pages 484

**The American Commonwealth** *by James Bryce*    ISBN: *1-59462-286-8*  **$34.45**
*An interpretation of American democratic political theory. It examines political mechanics and society from the perspective of Scotsman James Bryce*    Politics Pages 572

**Stories of the Pilgrims** *by Margaret P. Pumphrey*    ISBN: *1-59462-116-0*  **$17.95**
*This book explores pilgrims religious oppression in England as well as their escape to Holland and eventual crossing to America on the Mayflower, and their early days in New England...*    History Pages 268

QTY

**The Fasting Cure** by *Sinclair Upton*                                        ISBN: *1-59462-222-1*   **$13.95**
*In the Cosmopolitan Magazine for May, 1910, and in the Contemporary Review (London) for April, 1910, I published an article dealing with my experi-ences in fasting. I have written a great many magazine articles, but never one which attracted so much attention...  New Age/Self Help/Health Pages 164*

**Hebrew Astrology** by *Sepharial*                                        ISBN: *1-59462-308-2*   **$13.45**
*In these days of advanced thinking it is a matter of common observation that we have left many of the old landmarks behind and that we are now pressing forward to greater heights and to a wider horizon than that which represented the mind-content of our progenitors...  Astrology Pages 144*

**Thought Vibration or The Law of Attraction in the Thought World**          ISBN: *1-59462-127-6*   **$12.95**

by *William Walker Atkinson*                                                                *Psychology/Religion Pages 144*

**Optimism** by *Helen Keller*                                        ISBN: *1-59462-108-X*   **$15.95**
*Helen Keller was blind, deaf, and mute since 19 months old, yet famously learned how to overcome these handicaps, communicate with the world, and spread her lectures promoting optimism.  An inspiring read for everyone...  Biographies/Inspirational Pages 84*

**Sara Crewe** by *Frances Burnett*                                        ISBN: *1-59462-360-0*   **$9.45**
*In the first place, Miss Minchin lived in London. Her home was a large, dull, tall one, in a large, dull square, where all the houses were alike, and all the sparrows were alike, and where all the door-knockers made the same heavy sound...  Childrens/Classic Pages 88*

**The Autobiography of Benjamin Franklin** by *Benjamin Franklin*          ISBN: *1-59462-135-7*   **$24.95**
*The Autobiography of Benjamin Franklin has probably been more extensively read than any other American historical work, and no other book of its kind has had such ups and downs of fortune. Franklin lived for many years in England, where he was agent...  Biographies/History Pages 332*

| Name | |
| --- | --- |
| Email | |
| Telephone | |
| Address | |
| | |
| City, State ZIP | |

☐ **Credit Card**          ☐ **Check / Money Order**

| Credit Card Number | |
| --- | --- |
| Expiration Date | |
| Signature | |

*Please Mail to:*   Book Jungle
PO Box 2226
Champaign, IL 61825
*or Fax to:*          630-214-0564

## ORDERING INFORMATION

**web**: *www.bookjungle.com*
**email**: *sales@bookjungle.com*
**fax**: *630-214-0564*
**mail**: *Book Jungle  PO Box 2226  Champaign, IL 61825*
**or PayPal** *to sales@bookjungle.com*

*Please contact us for bulk discounts*

## DIRECT-ORDER TERMS

**20% Discount if You Order
Two or More Books**
Free Domestic Shipping!
Accepted: Master Card, Visa,
Discover, American Express